Whisper of Evil

WHISPER OF EVIL

J.H. Rhodes

AVALON BOOKS
THOMAS BOUREGY AND COMPANY, INC.
NEW YORK

Library of Congress Catalog Card Number: 85-61890
ISBN 0-8034-8519-0

PRINTED IN THE UNITED STATES OF AMERICA
BY HADDON CRAFTSMEN, SCRANTON, PENNSYLVANIA

Whisper of Evil

Prologue

For the first time since she had lived at The Towers she was frightened. She hadn't wanted to go to the east wing today, but there was nothing she could do about it. That was the trouble with getting old and being confined to a wheelchair. She had never been one to voice her opinion; she had, as long as she could remember, been a quiet, introverted person.

Her husband had always tried to get her to stand up for herself. But she had always relied so much upon him. He had given her strength through all the years they had been married. Now, with him gone, that strength somehow seemed to vanish too.

Brandon had insisted they go for a "wheel-walk" as he liked to call it. At first it had seemed like a good idea. She loved Brandon, even though he was too much like her, too much so for his own good. Then when they came to the east wing and that awful staircase that suddenly terrified her, she wanted to turn around and go back to the safety of her own room.

Why did she feel this way? She had been in the east wing many times and had never felt this uneasiness before. But today, for some reason, there was danger in the air.

Had she seen a shadow back there where there should not have been one? Or was that just her imagination? Probably so. This past year she had imagined all sorts of things. The doctor had said that was because she was not getting enough exercise. What else could he expect? He was the one who had confined her to her bed.

There! She knew that someone was following them. Should she tell Brandon to go back? There was danger here in the east wing. He went somewhere. She tried to turn her head far enough to see where he had gone. Those stairs, those dreadful stairs, right ahead of her. Yes, there was danger in the air.

Someone was behind her now. Brandon must be back. She would speak to him about leaving her alone. Not harshly. She couldn't do that to Brandon. Well, here was Brandon behind the chair. Or was it? She was getting confused again.

The chair was moving now, moving too close to the stairs. Her heart began to pound furiously in her chest. She was frightened. She mustn't get too close to the stairs. It was too dangerous.

Chapter One

"You have to be the world's greatest optimist," Marcie Clovis said to her best friend, Jane Stewart, as they sat in the Stewart living room sipping diet colas from tall, frosted glasses.

Jane laughed. It was a warm, deep-throated laugh that was so surprising coming from someone as small as she was.

"So I'm an optimist, am I?" Jane said, smoothing back her blond hair. She had known Marcie Clovis ever since babyhood and they were as close as sisters.

"What else? Anybody else by this time would be a mass of depression," Marcie said and then took a quick sip of her drink.

Jane stared at her friend and saw a lively brunette with short brown hair neatly trimmed in bangs across her forehead. Marcie was the optimist, Jane thought as she studied her lively, peppy girlfriend.

"You mean my twisted ankle," Jane said as she studied her right foot. "But that's almost well now. I'm good as new."

"Well, it couldn't have happened at a worse time," Marcie replied. "You haven't heard anything more from Mr. Jason, have you?"

Mr. Jason was the owner of the auto sales company in the heart of Big Bow, the small town in Colorado where Jane and Marcie had been born and reared.

"Not since he called and offered me the job, which I had to refuse because of the accident," Jane said with a sigh. "And I don't blame him for not waiting for my ankle to get better. He needed someone right away for the counter job. I couldn't very well have stood on my feet for eight hours with a twisted ankle."

Marcie agreed, then asked, "You haven't given up jogging for good because of what happened, have you?"

"For the time being only. When I'm sure that my ankle is perfectly healed, I'll start again."

"There aren't a lot of jobs here in Big Bow," Marcie said as she finished her drink. "I was lucky that my dad owns the drugstore. Anyway, maybe it's a blessing that you didn't get the job with Mr. Jason."

Jane stared inquisitively at her friend. She wasn't sure that she had understood what Marcie was saying.

Marcie soon continued. "Well, you're not like me, Janey. I'm perfectly content to spend the rest of my life here in Big Bow. But I think you need to get away, to see other places."

"Where did you come up with that idea?"

"From you," Marcie said, quickly getting another can of soda from the kitchen. "Remember when we were younger? You always talked about going to faraway places and seeing interesting sights and meeting all kinds of new and different people."

Jane laughed. "That was a long time ago."

"Maybe. But can you tell me that you wouldn't jump at the chance for a job in another place?"

"I would. But I'm not very likely to get one," Jane said and almost sighed at the dismal prospect of remaining in this small town for the foreseeable future. She had recently graduated from junior college and she planned to work and save money for a year or two before continuing her education.

"Who knows?" Marcie replied, her bright eyes flashing with interest. "Right at this very minute someone somewhere might be just longing for someone like you to work for them."

That really brought a chuckle from Jane. "For a minute there, I was almost going along with your plans for my future. However, there is something exciting going to happen. Today, as a matter of fact."

"Tell me!"

"Randy's coming home for a visit."

Randy was Jane's older brother. He, at least, had left Colorado. After he graduated college, he got a job with a company that made electronic equipment and he traveled all over the country as a sales representative. Randy and Jane got along not only as brother and sister but as friends. Marcie had never made it a secret how she felt about Jane's brother.

"Do you think he'll call me?" Marcie asked with the eagerness of a little child.

"Doesn't he always?" Jane replied, an amused

smile on her lips. "Randy thinks a lot of you."

They discussed Randy for about a half hour and then Marcie glanced at her wristwatch and said that she had to get to work.

"I'll be in touch," she called as she hurried out the front door.

Now that Jane was alone, she leaned back on the pillow of the sofa and thought about what had been happening to her for the past few weeks.

First there had been the accident. In a way it had been her fault. She hadn't been watching where she was going when she was out jogging. She had been wearing her headset and listening to one of her favorite tapes and not looking at the road. When she had stepped into a hole, she had twisted her ankle. Thank heavens she hadn't been jogging on the road alone.

The man who had been following her had helped her to his car and then taken her to the hospital. He had really been concerned and thoughtful. After the doctor had taped her leg and given her strict instructions to remain off it, she had been taken home by her fellow jogger.

"Janey, what happened?" her mother had asked with such anxiety in her voice that Jane had felt sorry for her.

"I took a tumble while I was running," Jane had answered. "Dr. Gifford told me to elevate my foot and stay off it for a while."

Both Jane and her mother had thanked the other jogger for his kindness and thoughtfulness and he had said, "Guess I was just in the right place at the right time. We joggers have to look out for each other."

When he had gone and Jane had settled herself on the sofa, her mother had brought her a cup of tea. Jane's mother always thought that tea was the greatest healing agent in the world. And sometimes Jane had to agree with her.

"Is it very painful?" her mother had asked as she placed the cup and saucer on the coffee table next to the sofa. "You look worried."

"It's that job I applied for at Mr. Jason's place. It would be just terrible if he called now and offered me that job. I couldn't possibly accept it."

In an hour Jane's worst fears were realized. Mr. Jason did call and she did have to refuse the offer.

"It's all right," Jane's mother had said. "There'll be other jobs. Maybe you were just not meant to work for Mr. Jason."

It wasn't much consolation, but Jane tried not to show her disappointment in front of her mother. Jobs were just not that easy to come by here in Big Bow and she did want to work.

Losing the job with the auto sales company was not the only thing that had happened to Jane recently. One evening, after dinner, Dal Williams came by to see Jane.

Dal had been dating her for over a year. Even though he had been very casual about their relationship, Jane had thought that Dal really cared for her. And she had been fond of him despite the fact that he sometimes seemed stuck up.

After her mother and father had gone into the kitchen, presumably to play a game of cards, Dal stood somewhat nervously at the head of the sofa and looked down at Jane.

"You feeling any better?" he finally said.

"Oh, yes," Jane said. "I'll probably be able to climb Mt. Everest next week."

Dal did not smile. "Yeah, sure," he said in a flat tone of voice. "Well, you know me, Jane, I'm not one to beat around the bush. I just say what's on my mind and that's it."

Jane looked into Dal's eyes and saw that they were cold and unfeeling. She almost knew what he was going to say before it came out.

"Recently I've had some time to do some thinking about us," Dal began.

Now he'll tell me, Jane thought. He'll be direct, forthright, and crushing. She could almost read his thoughts. There was someone else. Dal wasn't the type of person who burned his bridges without some greener pastures on the other side of the water.

"Maybe we shouldn't be seeing so much of each other," he went on. "This isn't coming out the way I'd planned. Anyway, to be blunt, I've found someone else. Since you won't be available for a while, I can't just sit around without a date. You know how active I am."

Jane assured him that she knew that. "It's all right, Dal. I understand."

"You do? Say, that's really great. But to give you

some encouragement, when you get better, we can still go out sometimes. I'm sure my girl will understand."

Jane felt her hands tighten at her sides. "Sorry, Dal. Even if she did understand, I wouldn't. Maybe you'd better leave."

Dal's face got slightly red. "If you're going to take it that way, maybe I should. Just remember I gave you your chance."

After Dal had gone, Jane just lay there trying to keep her anger in control.

In a few days, however, she was almost thankful that Dal had come to see her. It was good to find out what he was really like. She was lucky to be rid of him even though she missed him a little.

Jane was jolted out of her reverie when the front door opened and a brown-haired bundle of electric energy came charging into the house. Randy swept her into his arms and swung her around the room as if she were a rag doll.

Then he put her down and said, "What's all this I hear about you twisting your ankle? You weren't break dancing, were you?"

Jane laughed and told her brother what had been happening to her since she'd graduated from junior college. Randy listened attentively; he had always cared about Jane and her problems. When she had finished, their mother came into the room and the conversation was diverted from Jane to Randy.

It was later that evening while Jane and Randy and their parents were in the den sipping coffee that

Jane had a chance to speak at greater length to her brother.

"It's a pity you lost out on that job," Randy said. "But maybe I have another job for you. I don't know why I didn't think of you before. You would be perfect for it. Only, it's in Utah."

"Utah!" Jane exclaimed, her gray eyes sparkling. "Tell me all about it."

Randy settled back in his chair and said, "I met this man while I was in the northern part of the state. His name is Hugh Hammett. Seems that he has a small son that needs someone to look after him. The place he lives in is quite isolated, so it's difficult for him to find someone who would be interested in living there. He's hired some people, and they've quit."

Jane was listening intently. "But I'm not a tutor, Randy. I couldn't teach the little boy."

"That won't be necessary. Hugh Hammett just wants someone for a couple of months or so. And who knows? Maybe even longer, if you work out. You like kids. I know you do, sis, and that's the type of person he's looking for. Would you be interested?"

Jane thought for a moment and then said, "Well, it's the only offer I've had since Mr. Jason had to find someone else for his company. But do you think this Mr. Hammett would want me?"

Randy smiled at his only sister. "He would be a fool not to. The Hammetts live, from what he told me, in a huge house called The Towers. From what

I gathered, listening to Hugh speak, they are quite a wealthy family."

Jane's mother turned to her and said, "It sounds exciting. And I know you've always wanted to visit another state."

"What do you say?" Randy said as he leaned forward in his chair.

"I say I'll go for it," Jane said.

Yet even as she spoke those words, a feeling of uneasiness came over her. It was as though she were being warned not to go to The Towers because there was danger there for her.

Chapter Two

"Since I'm a man of action," Randy said as he got to his feet, "I'm going to call Hugh Hammett right now. Just in case he might have found someone since I last spoke to him."

Jane knew that she couldn't back out now, so she just watched as her energetic brother walked purposefully over to the telephone and began dialing.

Randy spoke for a few moments to somebody and then he turned to face Jane. "Mr. Hammett would like a few words with you."

Jane got to her feet and walked over to her brother. There was still time, a voice within her whispered, still time to turn down the offer.

Then Jane shook those thoughts from her mind as she took the telephone from Randy's hand.

"This is Jane Stewart speaking," she heard herself say.

"Miss Stewart, I'm Hugh Hammett. Your brother has spoken very highly of you. He tells me that you are interested in taking care of my son."

"It was all so sudden. But, yes, I would like to be considered for the position. I like children and they seem to like me too."

Jane hoped that she didn't sound as awkward as she felt.

"You could be just the person we are looking for. Brandon will be your sole concern while you are at The Towers," Hugh Hammett said in his deep, no-nonsense tone of voice. "When do you think you will be able to come to The Towers?"

"I'll have to pack and see about servicing my car. I can be on the road in two days. If that is satisfactory?"

"Perfectly," Hugh Hammett said. "I'll wire you some money to take care of your expenses." Then he mentioned a salary figure which Jane thought quite generous.

She listened intently and wrote down the instructions on how to get to The Towers. When Hugh Hammett had finished giving her those instructions, he said, "Very well, we'll be expecting you. We are most grateful, Miss Stewart."

With that, Hugh Hammett hung up.

Jane pivoted around and said, "I got the job! I could kiss you, Randy." And she did.

"Son, tell us more about this Hugh Hammett and this place called The Towers," their father said.

"The Hammetts, from the little I've gathered, are old money. They've lived in The Towers for quite some time. I've never seen the place, but I've been told it's quite a house. There was recently an accident or something. But Hugh Hammett didn't dwell on it when we were discussing the job. Anyway, Brandon, Hugh's son, will be Jane's responsibility."

"How old is the boy?" Jane's mother asked, gazing up from the sweater she was knitting.

"Seven or eight, I believe," Randy said. "That's about all I know. Now I wish that I'd asked more questions. Only, how was I to know that that chance meeting with Hugh Hammett would involve Janey?"

"Where do they live? I mean near what city or town in Utah?" their father asked.

"Mountain Pass is the closest town," Randy said. "Isn't that right, Janey?"

Jane glanced down at the slip of paper in her hand. "That's what Mr. Hammett told me. What's he like, Randy? I mean, what does he look like? He sounded so stern and serious on the phone."

"He's tall. About six foot three. Pretty ruggedly built, takes care of himself. And I'd say he was in his early thirties."

Jane asked, "What about his wife?"

"He's a widower. His wife died of pneumonia several years ago. But that's about as far as I can go. We didn't spend that much time together."

Jane sighed and then said, "What is your impression of him? Do you like Hugh Hammett?"

Randy thought for a moment. "I don't know. He wasn't the sort of person you form an instant opinion of. Hugh Hammett was somewhat guarded when I spoke to him. But you know me, Janey. I'm as open as the Grand Canyon. And I expect everyone else to be the same way. Hugh Hammett isn't exactly outgoing."

"Don't discourage your sister, Randy," their mother said. "Janey will find out what Mr. Hammett's like after she gets to this place . . . The Towers."

"I say let's drink to it," Jane's father said.

Then he went to the kitchen and brought back a bottle of apple cider and four glasses.

When he had filled the glasses, he said, "To Jane and her success in her new position."

Two days later, after many hours of driving, Jane pulled into a service station in the town of Mountain Pass. While her tank was being filled, she asked the old attendant the directions to The Towers.

He stared at her with unblinking eyes and said, "A nice girl like you surely don't have no business at that place."

Jane felt awkward under his unblinking gaze but told him that she would be working there. The old man shrugged and pointed out the way.

As Jane drove off, she glanced in the rearview mirror and saw the old man looking after her, shaking his head. That gave her an uncomfortable feeling. Then Jane quickly dismissed the feeling. She would not let him dampen her enthusiasm.

It was just at sunset that Jane saw the house in the distance. It was a huge place that seemed remote and unfriendly, isolated from the world on a hilltop. Jane took a deep breath and tried to quiet the uneasiness in the pit of her stomach.

Chapter Three

As Jane drew nearer to the house, she slowed down, glancing at the fence that surrounded the place. In the front there were elaborate iron gates.

Moving through the gates, which were now open, as though beckoning to her, she found herself on a long concrete drive that rose sharply toward the house like a carpet.

The Towers was built of stone and looked like a medieval castle that had somehow found its way to Utah. The surrounding lawn and gardens were carefully tended.

There was a man, obviously the gardener, still working on the lawn. As she passed him, she touched the brake on the car.

"Excuse me," Jane said in an awkward tone of voice. "This is The Towers, isn't it?"

The man was middle-aged, tall, and angular. His face was a network of wrinkles, but when he smiled, the smile made him look ten years younger.

"That's right. This is the Hammett estate. You must be the new girl. They're expecting you."

"Thanks," Jane said. "By the way, my name is Jane Stewart."

The man's smile continued to brighten his face.

"Raymond's the name. Just follow the drive up to the house. Like I said, you are expected."

At least he's friendly, Jane thought as she turned her attention back to the driveway. She should be thankful for that.

When she arrived at the house, she parked her car and got out. Jane stood there for a moment or two, gazing at the imposing structure. Now that she was up so close, it seemed to be more intimidating than before.

The house had been aptly named, for it had a tower on each end. Jane wondered as she walked toward the front door whether or not she would ever feel at ease in such a palatial house.

She lifted the heavy knocker—there didn't seem to be a doorbell—then let it fall and repeated the action again. Soon the door was opened and she found herself staring at a tall, thin-faced woman with her hair pulled back into a tight chignon. The woman's pinched mouth opened, and when she spoke, there was very little friendliness in her voice.

"You must be Miss Stewart. Please come in."

"Is Mr. Hammett in?" was all that Jane could say as she gazed around at the corridor with the high, vaulted ceiling.

"He is away at the present," the woman replied in the same dead, flat tone of voice. "We are expecting him later this evening. I am Mrs. March, Mr. Hammett's housekeeper."

"What a beautiful house this is," Jane said and found that the words seemed somewhat inadequate, just as she was beginning to feel somewhat inadequate under the hard gaze of the housekeeper.

"I'll have your things brought in. You'll be staying in the west wing. Your room will be near young Mr. Brandon's."

Do people actually speak this way? was all that Jane could think as Mrs. March spoke. Then she quickly shoved those thoughts to the back of her mind. She mustn't be too critical of the people she would be working and living with.

As she was standing there with Mrs. March, a slender, elegantly dressed woman with short-clipped dark hair came walking toward her. Jane thought the woman might be considered pretty if she didn't have such a serious, no-nonsense look to her face.

When she drew close to Jane, she stretched out her hand and said, "Good evening. You must be Miss Stewart. I'm Katherine Hammett, Hugh's sister."

Katherine's voice was neither friendly nor unfriendly. Her grip was quite strong and Jane resisted an impulse to wince as the woman exerted pressure on her fingers.

"I'm told by Mrs. March that Mr. Hammett isn't here," Jane said boldly, meeting Katherine's unblinking eyes.

For a moment there was a slight smile on Katherine Hammett's thin lips. "I'm very sorry about that. It was just some unforeseen business in Mountain Pass. Hugh asked that I meet you and make you feel at home."

"That was thoughtful of him," Jane said as Mrs. March passed by them on her way to somewhere in the vast house. "This is all so new to me, I guess I'm just a little bit nervous."

"Please don't be," Katherine said in a husky voice.

"Don't let The Towers intimidate you," came a male voice, and Jane turned slightly to see a blond, curly-haired man who had apparently been watching the two of them after emerging from a room in the hall. "Good old Hugh wouldn't like that."

Jane noticed a slight resemblance between the man's features and Katherine's. She assumed that whoever this man was, he must be some relation.

"Jane Stewart, this is David Hammett, my brother," Katherine said in an offhand manner.

"Hello, Mr. Hammett," Jane managed to say in what she hoped was a pleasant tone of voice.

"Please call me David," he said as a lazy smile touched his lips. "After all, we'll be seeing a lot of each other."

At that moment, from behind David, stepped a short woman with mouse-colored hair. The woman was pretty in her own way, but there was a haunted, worried look in her eyes. "David, I think we'd better go into the library."

"In a moment," David said rather brusquely. "Jane, this is my wife, Lorene. She keeps me on the straight and narrow."

"Hello, Lorene. I seem to keep meeting more and more people. I hope I can keep all of you straight."

Lorene just nodded to Jane and then she turned

to David. He shrugged his shoulders and followed her away.

Somewhat surprised at Lorene's possessiveness, Jane turned to face Katherine, whose face was a mask. "You mustn't pay any attention to Lorene. She's just an overpossessive person. Reba, would you show Miss Stewart to her room."

This last was directed to a rather pretty girl about Jane's age, who had soundlessly entered the corridor. She was wearing a black uniform with a white apron, but the somber colors did not detract from her open cheerfulness.

"Reba will show you where you will be staying. If you would like, I can have a tray sent to your room," Katherine said with practiced efficiency.

"That would be nice. I am rather hungry and I am anxious to see Brandon," Jane replied.

"He's right down the hall from your room," Katherine said. "Hugh thought that you shouldn't be too far from him."

With that, Katherine walked away and Reba came over to Jane.

"Your room is upstairs, Miss Stewart. We take the west stairs. I'm really glad to see you."

Jane smiled at the pretty girl who obviously meant what she was saying. At least the gardener and the maid were friendly.

"It's a big place, isn't it?" Reba said as they walked to the staircase. "Rhea is just crazy about The Towers. I'm not so sure that I am."

"Who's Rhea?"

"My sister," Reba said. "We're twins. You might say that we came as a package deal here to the house. Sort of double duty."

They both chuckled at Reba's remark, and Jane noticed how odd it sounded; laughter was apparently rather foreign to this place.

Jane saw there were two staircases.

"That second one leads to the east wing. But nobody stays in that part of the house anymore."

They were mounting the stairs now and Jane glanced up to see a beautiful woman descending. She had auburn hair and wide green eyes. There was a patrician beauty about her high cheekbones and delicate nose.

When the woman saw Jane, one eyebrow rose questioningly.

Reba immediately said, "Oh, Miss Kannon, this is Jane Stewart."

"Pleased to meet you, Miss Kannon," Jane said with a hesitant smile.

"You must be the new help that Hugh was speaking about," the woman said with a slight mocking smile on her lips. "Brandon's governess."

Immediately, Jane knew that she would never like this cold woman. But she did not want to make an enemy of her right off the bat. "That's right. Only, I would hardly call myself a governess. I hope I can be a friend to Brandon."

"Good luck, Miss Stewart," the woman said as she swept past them.

Reba and Jane did not exchange another word until

they had reached the second-story landing.

Then Reba just sighed and said, "Don't let her bother you, Miss Stewart. She treats all of the help that way."

"She didn't bother me," Jane said. "What did you say her name was? And is she another relative?"

"Her name's Helene Kannon. And she's not related to the Hammetts. She's what you might call a friend of the family."

They walked along the hall, which had many doors facing it. Jane was becoming more and more aware of just how huge The Towers really was.

When they came to her room, Reba opened the door and Jane went inside. The maid followed her. It was a lovely room with a canopied bed and an antique dressing table with a mirror. There were several chairs and other pieces of furniture scattered throughout.

"It's beautiful," Jane said as she glanced around.

"I'm glad you like it, Miss Stewart," Reba said. "Mr. Hammett picked it out himself. I hope you'll be comfortable here."

"Reba, why don't you call me Jane," she said to the maid. "At least when we're alone. I'm just not used to all this formality."

"I thought you would be like that," Reba said, a smile brightening her features. "We need someone like you here. Especially after what happened to Miss Dorothea."

Jane stared questioningly at Reba, who said, "That

is the Hammetts' mother. She had an accident. Her wheelchair went down the stairs in the east wing. It was just awful. Miss Dorothea was put back in her bed and she hasn't hardly spoken a word since. I guess it was the shock of it all."

"How terrible," Jane said, aghast. "How did it happen?"

Reba shook her head. "We aren't too certain. Brandon was with her when it happened, and he won't say anything. He's a strange little boy, but I think he just needs a lot of love and understanding."

At that moment there was a light rap on the door. When Jane opened it, she was taken aback for a moment. The girl who stood in the doorway with a tray in her hands was the exact duplicate of Reba. Only, there was none of the friendly, lightheartedness in her features that was so evident in Reba's face.

"Miss Katherine asked me to bring you this tray." Rhea glanced at Reba, and there was a narrowing of her eyes as she walked past her sister and put the tray on the dressing table.

"You'd better come with me, Reba. I'm sure Miss Stewart wants to eat her meal in quiet."

Reba glanced nervously from Jane to her sister and then obediently followed her twin out of the room. Jane knew that she would be able to tell them apart in the future. Reba was so warm and outgoing, while her sister was just as cold and unfeeling as most of the people she had met since she had arrived at The Towers.

While she was eating, her luggage was brought up by Raymond, who also brought some sort of warmth into the room with him.

"Raymond, before you go, do you know which room belongs to Brandon?"

Raymond glanced down the hallway and then said, "It's that one, Miss Stewart. The door's open just a bit. I think you'll be good for the tyke. He needs a friend."

Jane stared at the open door and then took a deep breath and walked down the corridor to Brandon's room. She rapped lightly and the door opened at her touch.

Walking in, she saw a young boy huddled deep in the covers of an outsized bed. He had dark hair and was almost angelic in appearance, except that his eyes stared at Jane.

"Hi!" Jane said as she moved cautiously toward the bed. "You must be Brandon. How's it going?"

Brandon just watched her with his wide-awake eyes, not saying a word.

"You know, I always wanted a little brother. My brother is older than me. Do you think maybe we can be friends?"

Not a word from Brandon.

"I think we're going to get along," Jane said, trying to put as much conviction into her voice as possible. She walked over to a lamp that was blazing on the nightstand. "Do you want me to turn this off? Or shall I just leave it on all night?"

At the mention of turning it off, she noticed a

look of fear in Brandon's eyes and she got the message. "Let's leave it on. Hey, I know a lot of games we can play tomorrow. Games my brother and I used to play. Would you like that?"

Jane noticed a slight flicker of interest in Brandon's eyes, and then that interest quickly faded.

"Okay, you think about it. If you need anything, I'll be in my room right along the hall."

Slowly pivoting, Jane walked to the door. When she left, she kept it slightly ajar, just the way she had found it. Walking back to her room, she was certain of one thing. Brandon either didn't like her or he was terrified of something.

Chapter Four

Returning to her own room, Jane opened the pieces of luggage and began hanging her things in the closet. She needed to do something with her hands. She always thought better when she was working.

This certainly was a strange household, Jane thought as she hung one of her dresses on a hanger. But after what Reba had told her, she could understand it a little. She wondered where the accident had occurred. Then she remembered that Reba had said it had been in the east wing. Perhaps that was why that wing of the house was not used. With the size of The Towers, all the people that she had met so far could live quite comfortably in this wing.

Maybe she shouldn't have come here, Jane thought as she moved from the luggage to the closet. There was an undercurrent here that bothered her. It was as though something very tragic had occurred and everyone was holding his breath, waiting for the next tragedy to occur.

"That's ridiculous," Jane muttered. "You've been watching too many thrillers on TV. You'll get used to this house and the people in it. Don't go imagining things that aren't there."

After this personal dressing down, Jane felt much better and she found that she was even whistling a faint little tune. Then she caught herself. Somehow, whistling, singing, and laughing seemed totally out of place here in this house.

There was a light rap at her door and, when she opened it, she saw Rhea standing there. Jane knew right off the bat that it was not her warm, friendly sister. Rhea's mouth was set in a firm, straight line.

"If you've finished with your supper, I've come for your tray," she said in a remote tone of voice.

"Yes, thank you," Jane replied. "It was very good. Only, I just wasn't as hungry as I should have been. How do you like living here at The Towers, Rhea?"

Rhea gave Jane a quick, searching look. "So you can tell me apart from my sister. Most people can't. Reba is a little too forward and friendly with the people here. I've told her not to mingle with the Hammetts. She should know her place."

"I don't mind her in the least," Jane said. "Your sister is a very lively and interesting person."

Rhea just gave Jane a stony look and walked out of the room. If ever two people were opposite in temperament, it was those two. Almost like night and day. Jane got the feeling that Rhea resented her twin.

Jane glanced at her wristwatch and saw that it was only eight-thirty. She was not tired. She was still keyed up from the long trip. Looking around the room for something to read, she found nothing.

Surely, in a house this size, there must be a library. She would find it and pick up something to read herself to sleep.

As Jane left her room, she glanced down the corridor and did not see anyone. The house was surprisingly quiet at this time of night, and she walked cautiously down the hallway. Once she glanced back, having the feeling that she was being watched, but there was nobody in the corridor.

As Jane approached the stairs, she glanced ahead of her to the east wing. It was in darkness. There was a forbidding atmosphere to that portion of the house. It was there that the accident had occurred. Her curiosity aroused, Jane took a step or two toward that part of the house.

"Looking for something, Miss Stewart?" a woman's voice asked and Jane turned quickly to see Katherine Hammett standing behind her.

"I was looking for the library," Jane said. "Since I wasn't particularly sleepy, I thought I might find a book to read."

Katherine's face was in shadows so Jane couldn't tell what expression was there.

"The library is on the ground floor. We never use the east wing any longer. Would you like me to take you to the library? I'm sure you'll be able to find something to read."

"If you would just tell me which room it is, I'm sure that I can find it," Jane said. "I don't want to put you to any trouble."

Katherine told her where the library was located,

and Jane thanked her and hurried down the staircase. She couldn't help but feel like a mischievous child who had been reprimanded by an older person.

Jane found the library easily enough. As she walked into the lighted room, she saw David Hammett sitting in an overstuffed chair with a book, opened but unread, in his lap.

"Well, this is a pleasant surprise," David said as his mouth twisted in a slight, mocking smile. "I take it that you came here to find a book and not to see me."

Jane did not like the way he spoke, and she felt uneasy being alone in the same room with Hugh Hammett's brother. She could still remember the look on Lorene's face when they had met earlier that evening.

"I just wanted something to read before I went to bed. Katherine told me where to find the library."

Jane walked over to the bookcase, which went from the floor to the ceiling. She reached out and took a book from the shelf in front of her. It was a volume of short stories by Mark Twain. She didn't especially feel in the mood for that sort of writing tonight, but she didn't want to remain in the room with David any longer than was necessary.

"You are easily pleased," David said as he shifted his position in the chair. "How do you find the house and the people who live here at The Towers?"

"It's too early to tell," Jane said as she met David's steady gaze.

"We're a peculiar family. Maybe it has something

to do with this house. Anyway, I wouldn't be roaming about in it at night until you get accustomed to it," said David as a slight smile once again touched his lips.

"I'd better get back to my room," Jane said, then turned and walked out of the library.

There was little doubt in her mind that David Hammett was an attractive man, and he was fully aware of his appeal. Jane made a silent resolution that in the future she would not allow herself to be caught alone with him.

Jane walked briskly toward the main corridor thinking about what David had said to her. Something about the family being peculiar and for her to be careful while she was in the house. As David's words echoed in her mind, she found that she had quickened her stride.

When she got to the head of the stairs, she heard a door open and she saw Helene Kannon emerge from her room. Helene saw Jane at the exact moment that Jane glanced in her direction.

"Everyone seems restless tonight," Helene said as she moved down the hallway toward Jane. "Even the hired help."

Jane felt her hands tighten on the book, but she didn't reply to Helene's obvious barb.

"And how is your little ward tonight? Or have you had a chance to see Brandon yet?"

"Yes, I've met him. It will take a little time before he trusts me," Jane replied, not allowing this woman to intimidate her. "He is just a little boy and he needs a lot of attention."

Helene glanced once in the direction of Brandon's room and then shrugged. "Good luck. You'll need it."

With those words, the beautiful woman swept past Jane as though she weren't there and walked gracefully down the stairs. Jane watched her for a moment and then walked the remaining distance to her room. There was one thing she was certain of: Helene Kannon was a first-class snob. She had met other women like Helene and she had never had much use for them. Helene probably came from a wealthy family and had been catered to all of her life. So far, outside of Reba and possibly the gardener, Jane hadn't met anyone at The Towers who was outwardly friendly.

Stepping into her room and closing the door behind her, she sighed and walked over to the bed where she dropped the book. She decided to shed her clothing and put on her pajamas. Then she would curl up in bed and try to concentrate on the stories.

Ten minutes later, Jane was in bed, with the book opened in front of her. Taking her eyes off the pages, she glanced around the bedroom. It made her own room back in Colorado seem very small by comparison.

She wondered if she would ever feel at ease in such an opulent, expensive room.

Then she shrugged and said, "Enjoy it, old girl. You don't know how long this job will last, so you might as well get the most out of it. Besides, you are the one who wanted to travel."

Before Jane tackled the book once again, she thought about Marcie Clovis and how the pert brunette would be bowled over if she were here now. Jane made a mental note to write to Marcie when she found the time the next day.

Once Jane got into the book, she found that Mark Twain could still weave his spell over her and she found herself eagerly turning each page until she had completed the short story she was reading.

Then she let the book drop to her side, and once again thoughts of the house and David Hammett and Brandon came rushing to her. David's words in the library had almost been a threat to her. Was The Towers really such an evil—or at least dangerous—place as he made it out to be? So far Jane hadn't met anyone outside of Raymond and Reba who had been even remotely civil to her.

Katherine Hammett had not been unkind, but rather just cool and distant. It was probably just the way she was, and Jane would have to accept her.

And what about the accident that had happened to Brandon's grandmother? What a terrible thing that must have been. Perhaps that explained, in part, why everyone at the house seemed so unusual, why there was such a tense atmosphere here.

Jane cast aside these thoughts because she didn't want to think so heavily before she went to sleep. There would be time tomorrow to ponder over the people who inhabited The Towers.

Picking up the book once more, she read until she found that nothing made sense. Her eyelids had become heavy, so she put the book on the nightstand and switched off the lamp.

Now that Jane was settled, she yawned and gave in to the fatigue that had begun to catch up with her. Yet her sleep was light. And when the sound came, she opened her eyes wide with alertness.

What had she heard? Was it just the foundation in this ancient house, or was it the wind that had suddenly sprung up? Jane lay there, every muscle tense and her senses alert. The sound did not repeat itself and she began to relax, thinking that she just hadn't gotten used to the new environment.

Just as she closed her eyes, the sound came again. This time Jane flung the covers aside and reached for her robe, which she had placed across the foot of the enormous bed.

Not bothering to slip into her slippers, she walked to the door of the room and opened it. Outside, the corridor was dark. Only one faint light was on far down the hallway. Standing outside her room, Jane was listening so intently that it was almost hurtful to her ears. She knew that she hadn't been mistaken. There had been a noise. Some sound, almost like a whimper. She couldn't be certain that it was a whimper—only that something had awakened her.

As Jane stood there, she heard it once again and she knew that it was coming from Brandon's room.

In the darkness of the hallway, she was glad that she had taken the time earlier to find out which room was Brandon's. And she rushed there now.

The door was ajar, just as she had left it, but the bedroom was in darkness. Someone had been in the room and had switched off the light.

Jane reached out and touched the door so that it opened.

"Brandon! It's me, Jane. Are you all right?"

Brandon's answer was again that terrified whimper that she had heard before. "It's all right. I'm here now."

As Jane moved toward his bed, she had the feeling that she and Brandon were not alone. But before she could turn on the lights, she felt strong hands thrust against her back and she fell headlong. She did manage a startled shriek just as her head struck something and she lost consciousness.

Chapter Five

Jane seemed to be swirling in a sea of darkness for a time and then there was a faint light that grew brighter and brighter. When she opened her eyes, she heard voices and was staring into the face of the most handsome man she had ever seen in her life. His neatly trimmed dark hair framed his slightly tanned face. His thick eyebrows hovered over his midnight-black eyes, which had a slightly narrow look to them.

"Are you all right?" he asked.

Jane sat up and raised a hand to her forehead. "I believe so. Who are you?"

"I'm the man who hired you to take care of my son," said Hugh Hammett. "We spoke on the telephone. You couldn't be anyone else but Jane Stewart."

"Miss Stewart arrived earlier this evening," said Katherine. "We didn't know that you would be so late in returning home, Hugh."

"The main thing is that I'm here now," Hugh said. "Just what happened here, Miss Stewart?"

"I'm not sure," Jane said, trying to recall just what had happened after she had left her room.

"Try to recall," Hugh said in a heavy tone of voice.

"I awoke and thought I heard a noise. When I came out of my room, it seemed to be coming from Brandon's bedroom. I remember walking over to his door and finding that his night light was off."

"It should have been," David Hammett said. "You spoil that kid of yours, Hugh."

Hugh Hammett flashed his brother a quick, angry look and then turned his gaze back to Jane.

She said, "When I came into the room, there was somebody else here. Whoever it was gave me a shove and I must have struck my head."

"You probably just tripped over something," Helene Kannon said. "After all, it was dark and the house is unfamiliar to you."

Jane tried to find Helene's face in the crowd that hovered above her. When she did, she saw a faint, smirking smile on the woman's lips. It was obvious that Helene did not believe her story.

"Are you feeling better?" Hugh said. "Or should we call a doctor?"

"That won't be necessary," Jane said as she got up. She found that she was unsteady on her feet and clutched at the nearest arm. It happened to be Hugh Hammett's.

"Good old Hugh," David said in a cynical tone of voice. "Always the gallant gentleman."

"That will be enough, David," Hugh said sharply. "I think you should all go back to your rooms. Apparently, Miss Stewart is all right. And Brandon hasn't been harmed."

"Oh, Brandon," Jane said. "I forgot all about him!"

Jane moved as swiftly to Brandon's bed as she could and found that the night lamp was once more turned on and the little boy lay with the covers pulled up to his chin. His wide, frightened eyes stared at Jane in an unblinking way. Jane felt a flood of pity and love for the boy that made her own problems seem quite insignificant.

"Are you all right?" Jane asked.

But Brandon did not answer; he just kept staring at her in that terrified way.

Jane heard the sound of movement behind her, and she realized that the other people were going back to their rooms as Hugh Hammett had suggested.

Then she heard Helene speak before she made her exit. "I'd like to talk with you, Hugh, before you go to your room. It's very important."

Hugh's voice took on a more gentle tone when he spoke to Helene. "Very well. Why don't you wait in the corridor? I would like to speak to Miss Stewart for a few minutes."

Jane sat down on the bed and quietly arranged the covers around Brandon, saying, "It's all right now. Nothing is going to happen to you, Brandon. Try to think about tomorrow and the good times we're going to have together. Remember what I told you about my brother?"

By this time, Hugh was standing next to her. "He won't answer you, Miss Stewart. He hasn't spoken very much since the accident. And, for that matter, neither has his grandmother."

Jane noticed that as Hugh spoke Brandon shifted

his gaze from her to his father.

"You haven't gotten off to a very good start as a companion for my son," Hugh said in a flat, level tone of voice. "You are a lot younger than I thought you would be."

Jane looked up at Hugh. "I can't help my age, Mr. Hammett. But whether you believe it or not, I'm going to be a friend to your son. I think we're going to get along just fine."

"That remains to be seen," said Hugh in a disbelieving voice. "At the moment, you haven't made the greatest impression, as far as I'm concerned."

Jane's head was aching dully from the fall she had taken, and she felt her anger beginning to rise. She knew that she had a temper, and sometimes she just couldn't keep it in total control.

"I don't intend to make an impression on you, Mr. Hammett," Jane snapped. "But I do care about this little boy here. He's been badly frightened and that's all that I care about."

Hugh Hammett was silent. His dark eyes glared at Jane for a moment, and then a faint smile played at the corners of his mouth. "We can discuss all this in the morning. At the moment, I think it would be a good idea for you to get some sleep."

Jane watched as Hugh walked over to the nightstand. He totally ignored the little boy, his son, who lay rigidly in his bed. Reaching out, Hugh made a gesture toward turning off the lamp.

"Don't do that," Jane said. "I promised Brandon that the light would stay on. As you can see, somebody came in here and turned it off before."

"Very well," Hugh Hammett said with a touch of annoyance in his voice. "For now I'll let the light stay on. But I'm not going to continue to put up with this sort of thing. Now I think you should run along to your quarters, Miss Stewart."

"I will later," Jane said stubbornly. "At present, I think Brandon needs me. I'll stay with him until he gets to sleep."

Hugh Hammett's dark eyes swept from Jane to his son and then back to her. "That's up to you. Good night, Miss Stewart."

Without another word, and without as much as touching his son, Hugh Hammett left the room. Jane's anger was still boiling inside her, but when she looked at Brandon and saw how frightened he still seemed, that emotion left her and she felt compassion for Hugh's son.

A short while ago, someone had been in this room besides Brandon. The night lamp was turned off—and whoever had done that had also given her that shove. She couldn't help but wonder who it might be. It hadn't been an accident, as Helene had inferred. Jane could still feel the pressure of those strong hands on her back as the person had pushed her down.

Brandon stirred in his bed and Jane held back the urge to reach out and touch him. She mustn't go too fast with him.

For the moment she knew that all she could give him would be her presence in the room, to reassure him that he wasn't alone. That reassurance, Jane thought, should have come from Hugh Hammett. When he had been in the room, he had acted as though he were totally indifferent to the little boy. Did Hugh Hammett blame his son for his mother's accident in the east wing? Apparently, that was the case.

Jane sat quietly gazing into Brandon's eyes. His eyelids were beginning to droop somewhat. It wouldn't be long before he was asleep, Jane thought as she smiled at the small body in the middle of the oversized bed.

Who had been here with him earlier? The possibilities were many, Jane thought, sitting so still that she might have been a statue. It could have been just about anyone in the house. From Hugh Hammett down to Rhea, the list was a long one. But the question was why? Why would anyone be so cruel as to come into this room and turn off the lamp? Who disliked the little boy that much? Disliked him to such a degree that he or she wanted to frighten him?

Jane didn't want to think about that now, since she had only arrived at The Towers recently and really did not know any of the residents that well. What she did know for certain was that Hugh Hammett did not like her, nor did he particularly care for his son. That last matter bothered Jane more than the fact that someone had pushed her down in the dark.

She wondered if she could remain here very long with Hugh Hammett having that sort of attitude toward his son.

Maybe it would be better if she just packed her things and left the following morning. She really didn't need all this. She could find another job someplace. Yet even as she had these thoughts, Jane knew that she would not leave The Towers until she had helped this little boy to become less terrified.

No, she would not be a quitter. That just wasn't her style. Regardless of what Hugh Hammett thought of her, she was determined to remain here at The Towers. Hugh Hammett would just have to either like that or lump it.

Looking down at Brandon, Jane saw that he had finally closed his eyes and was breathing easily and naturally. Jane sat there for a few moments longer to make certain that he wouldn't awaken, and then she got to her feet and walked cautiously out of the room.

She left the door to Brandon's room slightly open. If anyone tried to sneak in there again, she hoped she would hear him.

As Jane headed for her bedroom, she saw Reba walking toward her, a sympathetic look on her face.

"Miss Stewart, I heard there was some commotion in Brandon's room and I'm so happy that you spent that time with him," the maid said. "You weren't seriously hurt, were you?"

Jane was thankful that somebody seemed concerned about her. "Just conked my head on something in the room when I was pushed. Otherwise, I'm feeling just fine."

Reba's eyes widened. "Pushed? I didn't know someone pushed you!"

Jane didn't want to go through it all again, but she knew that Reba at least cared about her. So she told her the story.

Reba said, "That's terrible. You watch yourself while you are here. It could have been worse."

"What do you mean?"

The maid glanced anxiously around and quickly said, "I really can't say anything more. I've got to be going. Rhea always tells me that I talk too much and am too friendly."

Without another word, Reba turned and hurried away.

A short while later, back in her bed, Jane drifted off to sleep. But it was not a peaceful sleep. She had a frightful nightmare.

At one point Jane found herself alone in The Towers, and outside a violent storm was raging. Lightning flashed through the windows and the ear-splitting sound of thunder echoed throughout the huge mansion.

But it wasn't the storm that frightened her. It was something else. She suddenly realized that she was not alone in the house, that someone, someone unseen, was stalking her. She ran breathlessly from room to room until she came to the east wing.

Jane felt a terrible sense of danger as she moved

into that darkened portion of the house, and then she heard the sound of footsteps behind her. Just as she turned to see who might be pursuing her, she awoke.

Chapter Six

After Jane showered and dressed, she found that the nightmare had faded somewhat. Then, as she brushed her blond hair, she thought of other things.

Gazing at her reflection in the mirror, she knew that she certainly was no match in the beauty department against Helene Kannon. But what did that matter? After all, she wasn't interested in Hugh Hammett as Helene was. And Jane told herself she could never be interested in a man who was so indifferent to his son.

Glancing down the hallway, she saw Rhea with a tray entering Brandon's room. With brisk strides she hurried to the young boy's bedroom. The door was open and she stood there for a moment as Rhea walked over to the bed.

Sensing that she was being watched, the maid turned and looked at Jane with indifferent eyes.

"Brandon doesn't eat with the others," Rhea said almost defiantly. "It's Mr. Hugh's orders."

"I see," Jane said even though she really didn't. "Well, Brandon, I'll see you after breakfast. We have a lot of things to do today."

Brandon just stared at Jane, but she felt there was

less terror in his eyes than she had seen last night. That was encouraging.

As Jane started down the stairs, she felt the presence of someone behind her and turned to see a balding man of about sixty-five. His blue eyes, cool as a winter sky, stared at her like ice cubes.

"Good morning," Jane said. "I don't believe we've met. I'm Jane Stewart."

"You don't have to tell me that. I've heard about you," the man said in a surly tone of voice. "If we have to exchange names, I'm Edgar Carrol."

Jane was beginning to get used to the coldness of the people who lived at The Towers, and somehow she managed a bright smile.

"Where is breakfast served, Mr. Carrol? This house is so big, I haven't found my way around it yet."

Mr. Carrol grudgingly moved next to her and said, "I'm on my way there now. You can come with me."

To make conversation, Jane said, "This is such a beautiful home. Have you lived here long?"

"Not too long. Dorothea asked me to come visit her. Of course, that was before her accident. I've known Dorothea and her late husband for years. Now that I'm retired, I can go wherever I please."

As they entered the dining room, Jane paused. It was huge and awesome. A crystal chandelier hung from the ceiling above a rather long table. Along one wall was a sideboard, and Jane saw Katherine and Helene with plates in their hands, helping themselves to breakfast.

"Did you sleep well, Miss Stewart?" came a familiar voice from behind her, and she turned to find Hugh Hammett standing there.

Once again Jane was struck by his handsome features. A little smile would have done wonders for that stern face, however.

"As well as I do in a strange room," Jane said truthfully. "But I'll get used to it. The bedroom is really very lovely. Thank you for picking it out for me."

For a moment there was a slight flicker of warmth in Hugh's eyes and a faint smile touched his full, sensuous lips. At that instant Jane could see a remarkable resemblance between him and his son, Brandon.

His smile quickly faded as Helene Kannon came over to where they were standing. "Hugh, you must sit next to me this morning. I still have so many things to talk over with you. You will excuse us, Miss Stewart."

There was no mistaking the proprietary attitude that Helene Kannon displayed as she hooked one arm through Hugh's and led him away, but not before Hugh excused himself. Helene glanced back over her shoulder and the look in her eyes told Jane that she was in charge of Hugh Hammett, and there was to be no interference from Jane Stewart.

Jane walked over to the sideboard and took a plate. As she ladled scrambled eggs onto her plate, she thought, You don't have to worry, Miss Kannon. I'm not in the least bit interested in Hugh Hammett. But she wondered if this was really the truth.

Taking her plate to the table, Jane sat next to Lorene, who appeared to be more friendly this morning than she had last night. David was seated next to Lorene and seemed absorbed in his food.

"I'm so sorry about your accident last night, Miss Stewart," Lorene said. "It can't be much of a welcoming for you."

Jane touched the place on her head that she had struck when she had fallen last night, and it was just slightly tender. "I'm feeling fine now. It was Brandon that I was worried about."

"Brandon!" came the voice of Katherine from across the table. "Did I hear you mention his name?"

"Lorene and I were just discussing last night," Jane said, and Katherine appeared to be more than just a trifle interested in their conversation. "I was telling her that I was more concerned for his safety than I was with my own."

"Safety!" Helene said with a smirk. "Don't tell me that you believe that somebody actually attacked you while you were in Brandon's room? Really, what next!"

Jane ignored the woman even though she couldn't very well overlook the way she was fawning over Hugh and occupying his full attention.

"You don't really believe that someone was in Brandon's room last night, do you?" asked David, who was actually able to detach himself from his food for a moment or two.

"All I can say is that I left the night lamp on for

Brandon, and when I checked in on him later, it was out. When I came into the room, somebody was there and gave me a push."

"It was dark," Katherine said. "Isn't it possible that you just thought you might have been pushed?"

Before Jane could answer, Hugh spoke. "Let's just drop the subject for now. Miss Stewart, I would like to speak to you after breakfast. That is, if it's convenient for you."

"Of course," Jane said. There were a few things that she wanted to discuss with the head of the house also.

For the rest of the meal, there was polite conversation: talk about the weather, the political scene, and money. Especially money. Jane felt somewhat left out until she turned to face Lorene, who gave her an understanding smile.

In a low voice, David's wife said, "I know how you feel. But money seems to be of great interest to the Hammett family. Please don't feel that you're being ignored. They really don't mean to be rude."

Jane found that she had indeed misjudged David's wife and that she might be able to establish some sort of friendship with her.

After they had eaten, everyone but Jane and Hugh and Helene Kannon left the vast dining room.

Hugh turned to face the auburn-haired beauty next to him and said, "If you will excuse Miss Stewart and myself, Helene, we have some matters to discuss."

Helene glared at Jane, but when she turned to look

at Hugh, her face was all sweetness and light. "Whatever you say, Hugh. But don't forget we have a date to go for a walk later this morning. I do enjoy the outdoors and especially being with you."

Hugh nodded as Helene left the room.

Then he turned to Jane. "Let's go into my study."

Hugh Hammett's study was a cozy place with mahogany and leather furnishings.

Hugh took a seat behind his desk. "Please sit down, Miss Stewart. Or would you prefer that I call you Jane?"

"Jane would be fine. Being called Miss Stewart makes me feel like I'm years older than I am."

"Even though this house and the people in it may appear to be formal, we really aren't. If you wish, you may call me Hugh."

"Very well," Jane said, although she found what he said about informality difficult to believe. Maybe in time she would be able to call him Hugh comfortably.

"First off, I would like to apologize for my behavior last night, Jane. I'm not usually that rude to people."

"I understand."

"Do you?" Hugh said, and then a warm smile touched his lips, giving him a totally different appearance. Jane hoped that this man she saw smiling in front of her was the real Hugh Hammett—and not that forbidding, dour person she had met last night. "That's good, Jane. Because I was really thankful that your brother recommended you. I don't know him very well, but from the little I saw of him, I thought he was a person I could trust."

"Randy is very likable. At least, I think so."

Hugh chuckled at her remark. "You sound as though you come from a very close family."

"We are. All of us are open and frank with each other. I don't see how a family could be otherwise."

For a moment there was a slight shadow that threatened to change Hugh back to the dour person he had been before.

Then the shadow passed and he said, "Maybe I should explain what you've gotten yourself into by coming to The Towers. You see, my mother, Dorothea, has been confined to her bed for some time. In order to get around, we use a wheelchair. One of us was always with her. But most of the time it was my son."

At the mention of his son, Jane saw a slight change again come over Hugh. She even saw that his hands tightened into fists as he spoke.

"Brandon was with Mother that day she was in the east wing. He left her for a few moments and then, well, we'll probably never know what happened. But the wheelchair came hurtling down the stairs. I think it was pushed. My mother was not seriously injured, by some miracle, but she hasn't really spoken since that accident. Or maybe she has said a word or two, nothing more."

"I see," Jane said. "And what about Brandon? He seems so withdrawn."

"He hardly says anything. All we know is that

Brandon was with her when the wheelchair went down the stairs."

"And you think that your son is responsible?"

"What else can I think? Neither one of them will tell us anything. I'm left with no alternative."

Jane was about to say something when there was a light rap on the door and Katherine came in.

"Hugh, if you are finished, there is something important that I must discuss with you."

Hugh glanced at his sister and back at Jane. "We can talk later, Jane. Would you excuse us, please?"

"Certainly," Jane said as she got to her feet.

Walking past Katherine, she noticed that Hugh's sister was smiling at her vaguely. Perhaps she had misjudged the people at the house. She just might be able to get along with them, after all.

Leaving the study, Jane walked to the staircase. She saw Reba coming toward her with an armload of linens.

On an impulse, Jane said, "Reba, which room is Dorothea in?"

Reba paused for a moment and glanced around, then said, "It's the second room on your left as you walk down the hallway."

Thanking the maid, Jane hurried up the stairs and rapped lightly on Dorothea's door. Then she entered the room.

Dorothea was propped up in bed. Her white hair framed a lovely face. There were hardly any wrinkles. As Jane drew nearer, she could see the resemblance that all the Hammetts had to this old woman who lay there with her eyes closed.

Not knowing why she was so bold, Jane walked closer to Dorothea. If only the woman could talk or even write, perhaps they would have the answer to what had happened in the east wing.

Jane stood there for a moment or two gazing down at the woman. Jane could see that she must have been a real beauty in her day. She was still a lovely woman now.

Slowly turning, Jane walked to the door. Out of curiosity, she abruptly turned her head and saw that Dorothea had been watching her. When Jane's eyes met the old woman's, Dorothea quickly shut her eyes, as though she were dismissing Jane. Quietly Jane left the room.

Chapter Seven

For a moment, after Jane had left Dorothea's room, she stood there wondering if Hugh's mother had been watching her the whole time she had been inside. Perhaps she shouldn't have gone there, but she had only done so in an attempt to learn why Brandon was so withdrawn and frightened.

Thinking of Brandon, Jane quickly walked to his door, then rapped lightly before going inside.

Brandon was dressed and was standing by the window, looking outside. He turned when Jane entered the room.

"Hi, Brandon. Were you looking outside? It's really a nice day. Let's go out. What do you say?"

For an instant there was a flicker of interest on his face and he said, "Will you really play with me?"

"Sure. I promised you, didn't I? Come on. You don't want to stay inside on a nice day like this."

Brandon walked over to Jane and took a fleeting look at his room before he went out. Jane closed the door behind them and together they walked to the stairs. Jane saw that Brandon was hesitant to go down the steps. She instinctively reached out and took his little hand. Together they walked down.

When they reached the bottom, Brandon glanced

up at Jane and said, "Are you going to be here long? Nobody stays with me very long."

Jane smiled at him and said, "I'll be here as long as you need me."

"You sure you won't go away, like the others?"

"Of course, I'm sure. I like you, and I think we're going to be good friends."

A quick smile touched Brandon's lips. But it disappeared as Edgar Carrol walked toward them.

"I see that you have already taken over your responsibilities, Miss Stewart," the man said as his eyebrows drew together in a slight scowl. "I hope that Brandon doesn't turn out to be too much to handle."

Jane could feel Brandon's hand tighten in hers. "I don't think he will be. Brandon and I get along just fine. I'm sure that you have other things to do with your time. Right now Brandon and I are going outside and have a good time."

Edgar Carrol's mouth tightened in an angry line and he hurried past them and up the stairs.

Jane looked down at Brandon and said, "Let's go. We both need some fresh air."

When they got outside, Jane was pleased to see that the sun was shining down from a cloudless sky. It was warm and pleasant and Brandon seemed to share her enthusiasm for the day.

"Doesn't anybody ever take you outside, Brandon?" Jane asked as they strolled away from the house.

Brandon shook his head. "They're all too busy."

Jane wondered if that was really the reason. Could Hugh Hammett be too busy to walk with his son? But Jane thought she knew the answer to that. Last night in Brandon's room, she had seen how Hugh Hammett had felt toward his son. Did he really believe that this young boy could have pushed his grandmother down the stairs?

Jane tried not to think about that. After all, she had been here such a little while and she knew hardly anything about this young boy.

"Don't you have a pet?" Jane asked. "A puppy or a kitten?"

"Aunt Katherine doesn't like animals," Brandon said, as though that was reason enough for him not to have a pet. "Did you ever have a pet?"

Jane chuckled. "Oh, yes. Lots of them. If I wasn't bringing home a stray dog or a cat, my brother did. We had birds and fish and all kinds of things."

Looking at Brandon's face, Jane decided that she wouldn't continue to tell him about the animals she and her brother had kept when they were young. It wasn't fair to Brandon, and she didn't want him to feel left out.

Glancing down, Jane saw a smooth stone and she stopped and picked it up. "This will be perfect to play catch with. Only, we have to be careful when we throw it. Want to give it a try?"

"Okay," Brandon said without any enthusiasm. "If you want to."

"Sure, I want to," Jane said, afraid to ask if he had a ball in his room. She had hardly seen any toys in there—and she didn't want to make him feel bad by asking whether he had some stored away somewhere. "You stand right where you are, and I'll walk over here and throw it to you. You just catch it and throw it back to me."

Jane walked a short distance away and then turned. Brandon was just standing there with his hands at his sides. He apparently didn't know the first thing about playing catch. Well, Jane thought, he'll learn.

"Here it comes. You catch it now, Brandon," Jane said as she tossed the stone with an underarm pitch.

The pebble sailed through the air and Brandon made an effort to catch it, but he missed. Then he turned and scrambled after the fallen stone. When he picked it up, he turned and looked at Jane as if he didn't know what to do next.

"Now you throw it to me," Jane said. "Don't worry, I'll catch it."

Brandon awkwardly tossed the stone and Jane expertly caught it and said, "That wasn't half bad. You've got a pretty good arm there, Brandon."

"Have I?" Brandon replied, enthusiasm beginning to mount in his small body. "Throw it to me, Jane! I want to catch it! Throw it!"

Jane couldn't help but laugh at Brandon's high spirits and she again tossed him the pebble. This time Brandon had cupped his hands and he caught the stone and held on.

"That was good," Jane said. "You must have played this game before."

"No, I haven't, honest," Brandon said with wide,

expressive eyes, looking very much like his father.

Jane tossed the stone again and it flew higher than she had intended. Brandon made a valiant attempt to catch it, lost his balance, and toppled onto the ground. He sat up and looked at Jane with a bewildered expression on his face, and then he grinned.

"Come on, Brandon. Get the stone and toss it," Jane urged. "You're all right. A little dirt never did any harm to anyone."

Brandon scrambled to his feet and ran for the makeshift ball. He was so excited that he tripped and fell again. But he got quickly to his feet and began to run once more. By this time Brandon's clean clothing was soiled and there were smudges on his cheeks. Yet Jane could see he was happy.

"Just what is going on here?" asked a sharp voice.

Jane turned around to see Katherine standing there, her arms crossed over her chest.

Seeing his aunt, Brandon dropped the stone and hurried over to Jane, who put a protective arm around his shoulders.

"We're playing a little game," Jane said. "And I think that Brandon is enjoying himself."

"He looks like a ragamuffin," Katherine said with a disdainful air.

"He can always wash," Jane said. "And his clothes can be washed too. Besides, I think the air is doing him a lot of good."

Katherine relented. "Brandon is in your care. Hugh did hire you, and he has good judgment."

Not saying another word, Katherine walked away.

Jane reached down and took Brandon's hand. "Let's go for a little walk."

"Don't you want to play with the stone anymore?" Brandon asked, looking up at Jane.

"We can do that some other time," Jane said. "After all, I'm going to be here for some time. Besides, there are a lot of stones around here so we won't be short of balls."

That seemed to placate Brandon, and he walked willingly at Jane's side. She felt that she had made some progress with Hugh Hammett's son, that he had actually shown some interest in the game. That was a good sign. And he even allowed her to take his hand while they were walking.

Jane didn't question Brandon about anything that had happened to him last night or what had gone on the day he took his grandmother to the east wing. It was still too early for that.

First, Jane knew that she had to win his confidence. He was beginning to trust her, and she must not do anything to spoil that.

Parallel to the sloping driveway were steps leading to the front gate. For a moment they both paused at the head of the stone steps, and then Jane boldly began to walk down them. Brandon hesitated just for a moment and then he walked beside her.

"I wonder how many steps there are here?" Jane said. "Have you ever counted them?"

"There are a lot of them," Brandon said. "Do you want to count them?"

"If you'll help me."

"Okay. Bet there are at least a hundred, maybe more."

"Bet you're right," Jane said with a slight touch of laughter on her lips.

They made a game of it. The faster they walked, the faster they counted. By the time they neared the bottom of the stairs, they were practically running. Brandon even giggled when they reached the sixtieth step, the last one. He did not seem to mind there were only sixty steps.

"That was fun," Jane said. "But let's rest for a few minutes."

Brandon sat next to her on the steps, and the scene seemed very peaceful.

After a few minutes, Jane said, "Time to move on. Are you rested, Brandon?"

Brandon shook his head. The camaraderie they had established only a brief time ago was suddenly gone. Jane began to walk up the driveway and Brandon came reluctantly along with her. She knew that she couldn't reach for his hand because that was not what he wanted at this moment.

Instead, Jane just walked slowly along, taking in the beauty of the surrounding scenery. In the distance, she saw Raymond at work. He waved a friendly greeting to her and she waved back. Glancing down, she saw that Brandon had lifted one hand and was also waving at the gardener.

When they neared the mansion, Jane saw David

Hammett standing outside. Seeing the two of them, David walked a short distance toward them and then paused.

"You two look as though you've been rolling in the dirt," David said.

Brandon moved closer to Jane and she managed a smile at Hugh Hammett's brother.

"Brandon and I were just playing a little game. Then we went for a walk."

David ignored Brandon and flashed Jane an expansive grin. He was not totally without charm, but Jane was definitely not interested in Lorene's husband.

"You surprise me, Miss Stewart. I never took you for the outdoor type."

"Looks can be deceiving," Jane said. "One shouldn't prejudge a person."

"True," David said as he raised a thick blond eyebrow. "I hope that you remain here long enough for the two of us to get acquainted."

Jane did not care for his insinuations, but she did not wish to make an enemy of Hugh Hammett's brother. "Oh, I intend to remain here a while. There are a lot of things that Brandon and I have to do."

"Oh, yes, Brandon. Just keep your eye on that one. He's not to be trusted."

Jane was about to protest when Lorene came out of the house. She stood there for a moment, looking at her husband and Jane, then said, "David, Katherine would like to speak to you."

David turned to face his wife and said, "I'll be

right there." Then he faced Jane and made a slight shrug with his shoulders. "Some other time, Miss Stewart."

Lorene waited until David had come to her, and then she followed him inside without one word to Jane.

Glancing down at Brandon, Jane saw that he wore an expressionless mask. How cruel his uncle had been to say such things in front of him. Jane quickly decided that she had to snap Brandon out of his mood.

"I'll race you to the house," she said. "Bet I can beat you."

Brandon looked up at her with blank eyes and then her challenge began to sink in.

His eyes brightened with excitement and he said, "Bet you can't!"

"At the count of three," Jane said. By the time she had counted the last number, Brandon was away and running.

Jane followed him thinking that she had won this match. But how many more would she win?

Chapter Eight

Once Jane and Brandon were inside the house, the boy went up the stairs to his room. Jane followed him. The house and the room had a strange effect on Hugh Hammett's son. He was once again the withdrawn child that she had met yesterday. It was as though they had never even been outside.

"Why don't you wash your face, Brandon?" Jane said. "While you're doing that, I'll go to the library and see if I can find a book we both can enjoy. Would you like me to read to you?"

Brandon didn't look at Jane as he walked toward the bathroom. "If you want to," was all he said.

Jane wasn't discouraged by Brandon's lack of interest. She knew that a good story would perk up his sagging spirits. All she had to do was give him time and he would come around to acting more like a normal little boy.

"I'll be right back," Jane called as she walked to the door and went into the hallway. As she walked, she glanced into the wide mirror that was on the wall. Then she looked to her right and saw that she could see into the mirror from her own room if the door was open. The hall mirror ran practically the length of the wall and was squeaky clean, probably due to the industry of Rhea.

When Jane reached the bottom of the stairs, she headed in the direction of the library, hoping that she would be alone there and wouldn't meet David Hammett as she had last night.

She breathed a sigh of relief when she entered the room and found it unoccupied. Going to the tall bookshelf, she found a book of adventurous folk tales and fairy tales that were bound to appeal to Brandon.

Jane had opened the book and stood there browsing through it when she felt the presence of someone at the door. Glancing up, Jane saw Helene Kannon standing there, staring at her.

"You seem to know your way around the house," Helene said in her imperious tone of voice.

"Katherine told me where the library was," Jane replied in a friendly tone. "There's certainly a fine collection of books here."

"Everything is first-class here at The Towers," was Helene's reply. "I watched you out the window when you were playing with Brandon. It won't do any good, you know."

"What do you mean?" Jane asked.

"Brandon, of course. He's a terrible little monster. Frankly, I believe he should be sent away. You really don't think you are doing him any good, do you?"

Jane could feel herself bristle at the cruel words Helene had spoken. How could she call Brandon a little monster? He was just a misunderstood and unloved boy.

"How can you say such things about Brandon? Given the right attention and affection, he'll be a warm and affectionate child."

"And I suppose you think you are the person who can accomplish these miracles?"

"I can try," Jane said.

A mocking smile touched the beautiful but cold features of Helene Kannon. "You do that. But I would suggest that you confine your interest to the son and not the father. I think it's only fair to tell you that Hugh and I will probably be married someday. I thought you might be interested in knowing that."

So that was Helene's real reason for coming into the library, Jane thought. Well, she shouldn't have bothered.

"Then you are engaged," Jane said in a level tone of voice. "I don't see a ring on your finger."

Helene said, "That will come."

"Are you sure?" Jane said, not caring whether or not she was upsetting Helene.

"Yes, I am sure. And I am also certain that I don't want you to have anything to do with Hugh."

"That hardly seems possible since he's my employer," Jane said calmly.

"Just you remember that. I want you to stay away from Hugh. That's all I have to say to you."

With those words, Helene swept out of the room, leaving Jane staring after her. She vowed not to let the arrogant beauty disturb her. After all, she was here to help Brandon—and she would focus on that.

On leaving the library, Jane ran into Reba. She asked the friendly maid, "Tell me something about Brandon. Doesn't he ever eat with the rest of the people in the house?"

Reba shook her head. "Not anymore. And isn't that terrible! I often bring him a tray of food. I try to stay with him as long as I can so that he'll eat something."

Jane sighed deeply. "From now on, I'll at least have lunch with him. Why isn't he allowed to eat in the dining room?"

Glancing around, almost as though she were afraid that she was being watched, Reba whispered, "It's because of what happened in the east wing. After the incident, Miss Katherine told me and my sister to take his meals to him. She said it was Mr. Hugh's orders. Only . . ."

"Yes?" Jane said, urging the maid to go on. "Only what, Reba?"

"It just didn't seem like the sort of thing that Mr. Hugh would ask. Of course, I'm just one of the help, so I do as I'm told. I said something to my sister, but she told me that she knew for certain that Mr. Hugh had told Katherine that. So I had to take her word for it."

Jane shook her head in dismay as she listened.

"I couldn't help but see you and Brandon outside," Reba said. "He seemed to really enjoy himself. It's about time he started acting like a little boy and not some hermit. You're going to be good for this old place, Jane. I, for one, am glad that you came here. I just hope that nothing happens to ruin all that you've done."

"Do you think something might?"

"I don't know," Reba said as she glanced anxiously around. "Sometimes this old house gives me the creeps. Although I really do like my job here. And Rhea likes it even more than I do. They must pay her more than they do me because she left her savings book out once and I saw the total. It was really something. But then Rhea works harder than I do, so I'm not complaining."

Jane seriously doubted that Reba's sister worked any harder than Reba, but she did not comment on this.

"I'd better get on with my work," Reba said. "Don't worry about lunch. I'll bring your food to Brandon's room."

Thanking Reba, Jane walked toward the staircase. Then she glanced at the grand piano that stood in the room nearest the stairs and strolled over to it. She idly touched a few keys and found that the piano was badly in need of tuning.

"Do you play, Jane?" Hugh asked.

She turned toward him and saw a slight scowl on his face.

"Just a little. Mostly what I pick up by ear," Jane replied. "It's a fine piano, but it really does need tuning."

The scowl slowly crept away from Hugh's features, and a slight smile tugged at the corners of his full, sensuous lips.

"My wife used to play. She was very talented," he said, and there was a wistfulness to his voice. "After she died, the piano was never played. I'm afraid that it has been sadly neglected."

"That's too bad," Jane replied. "Maybe it could be tuned and Brandon could be given lessons. It's a shame to let a beautiful instrument like that go to waste."

At the mention of Brandon's name, Jane saw the scowl once again cloud Hugh's features. "I have work to do. And I'm sure that you and Brandon have things to discuss."

"I thought I would read to him for a while," Jane said. "Do you think he'll enjoy these stories?" She held the book out to him.

"I leave that up to you."

With those words, Hugh turned and walked briskly into his study. There was a strange, unexplainable feeling in the pit of Jane's stomach. Hugh was certainly an irritating man—an unkind father—and yet she found him oddly magnetic. Oh, blast him!

Taking the book, Jane walked up the stairs, thinking about Hugh and his wife. Randy had told her that Hugh Hammett was a widower, that his wife had died of pneumonia several years ago. Jane felt sorry for Hugh, but she also wondered how he could be so neglectful of his son.

When Jane reached Brandon's room, she cast aside these thoughts and gave all her attention to the boy.

Brandon was sitting by the window looking longingly outside.

"Come on, Brandon, let's get on the floor and I'll read to you," Jane said, matching her actions to her words.

At first Brandon was hesitant, and then a quick, mischievous smile touched his lips and he dashed across the room and sat next to Jane.

"Have you read this book?" she asked.

Brandon shook his head.

"Then you are in for a treat," Jane said as she opened the volume and began to read.

Brandon listened carefully. Now and then Jane glanced at him and saw that he was entirely wrapped up in a story. She wondered how long it had been since anyone had taken the time to read to him.

The reading came to a halt when Reba brought them sandwiches.

"What do you want to do now?" Jane asked when they had finished eating.

"Read to me some more. Please, Jane?" Brandon pleaded, his eyes filled with anticipation.

"If that's what you want. I'm glad that you like the book," Jane replied as she reached for it once more.

For the rest of the afternoon, Jane read to Brandon, who seemed to never tire of the various stories.

When dinnertime approached, Jane reluctantly told Brandon that she had to leave him for a little while.

"Will you be back?"

"Of course, I will," Jane said. "I have to change for dinner. And I'll see you later. Why don't you play with those ships your father gave you?"

The miniature clipper ships stood on a small table in one corner of the room. Jane had assumed that they were a gift from his father. Brandon looked at them and then back at Jane.

"Go ahead, Brandon. That's what they're for, to play with. Use your imagination."

Brandon seemed to like the idea, and Jane left the room with the assurance that he would be all right for a brief time. At least until she had finished dinner.

Back in her room, Jane showered and put on a fresh dress. When she was fully attired, except for her shoes, she opened the door just in case Brandon might call out to her.

She found a pair of shoes that would complement her dress and she sat down on one of the chairs to put them on. As she sat there, she happened to glance out the door and she saw Rhea's reflection in the mirror. Reba's sister was standing close to the mirror but so intent on what she was doing with the tray in her hand that she did not see Jane watching her.

There was a small box that was on the tray and Rhea slowly opened it. It was very plain, but there were initials on the lid that were easily read, though they were backward. Jane stared in fascination at the box and the initials, H.K., which were clearly discernible even from this distance.

Rhea reached into the box and took something out

and then dropped it into the glass of milk that was on the tray. The maid then quickly slipped the box into a pocket of her apron and turned away from the hall mirror. Jane watched as Rhea took the tray into Dorothea's room.

Chapter Nine

After Rhea had gone into Dorothea's room, Jane sat there with her shoes in her hand, thinking about what the maid had done and the initials on the box. H.K. could only stand for Helene Kannon, but what had she to do with the maid or with Dorothea, for that matter? What had Rhea put in the old woman's milk? Was it some medication, or was it something deadly?

Jane brought her attention back to her shoes and quickly put them on. She sat on the chair quietly, waiting for Rhea to leave. It seemed like an eternity before she saw Rhea's reflection in the hall mirror as she left Dorothea's bedroom.

When Jane felt that enough time had elapsed, she got to her feet and walked out of her room, shutting the door behind her. She gazed down the corridor, but she did not see Rhea. Apparently, the maid had gone downstairs. Jane walked toward Dorothea's room and tried to drum up enough courage to go inside, but she simply couldn't, not now.

It was just as well that she had decided not to see Dorothea at this time because David and Lorene emerged from their room and came walking toward the staircase.

"It's refreshing to have a new face in the house," David said. "We're on our way to dinner."

"Won't you join us, Miss Stewart?" Lorene said in a friendly tone of voice.

"Of course," Jane replied as she walked over to Lorene's side. "But please call me Jane."

"Well, Jane, I was happy to see you and Brandon outside today. I think that was wonderful. That boy stays indoors too much. I don't think it's healthy for him to coop himself up in his room like he has been doing."

"We enjoyed ourselves," Jane said.

"I think you'll be good for this place," Lorene said, making it the second time today that Jane had heard those words.

"Thank you," Jane replied. "I'll do my best for Brandon. Actually, we seem to get along very well together."

There was a slight snorting sound from David. "If you do, then you'll be the only one. Did my dear brother tell you about the other girls who were here before you? They didn't last very long."

Jane tried to ignore the sarcasm in David Hammett's voice, although it wasn't easy. "I can't speak for the others, but so far I haven't had any trouble with Brandon."

"It's early yet," David said. "After all, you've only been here one day. Just give Brandon time."

"Oh, David, don't be that way," Lorene said in a pleading tone.

"Don't tell me how I should behave," David said

sharply, and Jane could see that Lorene almost seemed to shrink under his harsh tongue.

Lorene, she felt, was a very sensitive woman, and David was a tyrant.

"That's a lovely dress you're wearing, Lorene," Jane said, and David's wife looked at her in a grateful way.

"Lorene does have taste. I will say that," David said, the sarcasm not quite as venomous as it had been before. "I made certain of that before we married."

"Just what sort of work do you do, Mr. Hammett?" asked Jane as she looked at David over Lorene's somewhat bowed head.

"I'm afraid that all my mother's well-intended efforts to get me educated for some useful work did not pan out. I've been to the best schools and yet I'm not equipped to do anything, really. But why should I bother when there is no need to work? I'm quite comfortable living here at The Towers. Meanwhile, my talented brother keeps increasing the family fortune by making very astute investments."

Jane's distaste for David was mounting by the minute. He was obviously a spoiled, conceited person who was too lazy to work. Just the sort of person she did not have much patience with.

By this time, they had reached the dining room. When Jane glanced at the long table, she saw Hugh Hammett sitting at the head of it. He gestured to her with one hand, indicating that he would like Jane to take a seat on his right. Of course, Helene Kannon had managed to seat herself on his left.

"You look very lovely tonight, Jane," Hugh said as he pulled out her chair for her.

Glancing across the table, Jane couldn't help but notice the look on Helene's face. Her wide green eyes narrowed into slits, and there was a frozen smile on her lips.

"It really isn't fair, you know," David remarked after he had taken a seat. "You, dear brother, always manage to seat yourself with the prettiest people."

Jane glanced at David and Lorene and saw the look on Lorene's face, almost as though she wished that she were anyplace else but at the table. A pang of sympathy surged through Jane for David's wife.

"You are the lucky one," Hugh said. "You've found yourself an adoring and adorable wife. I would think that would be enough to satisfy you."

Jane saw the faint smile that touched the lips of David's wife, and she was thankful to Hugh for being so kind.

"That's right, David," Helene said. "Someday your brother will also find just the right person. Maybe sooner than you think."

"What's all this talk of marriage?" Edgar Carrol said as he unfolded his napkin and placed it across his lap.

Before Hugh could reply, Mrs. March entered the room and whispered something in his ear. Hugh listened intently.

"Excuse me, I have a phone call," he said when

the housekeeper had left. "Just go on without me."

There was a brief, awkward silence, and then Helene picked up the conversation, deliberately ignoring Jane.

It was Lorene who directed the attention to Jane at one point by saying, "What do you think, Jane?"

Jane quickly gave her answer to the question they had been discussing. She was very pleased and relieved when Hugh came back into the room.

"Anything important, Hugh?" asked Katherine, who had been very quiet while he had been out of the room.

"Just a business call," replied Hugh, reaching for his glass of iced tea and taking a sip. He made a slight face, since it had grown lukewarm.

"Hugh, dearest," said Helene, reaching out and pushing her glass toward him, "take my tea. It's still cold."

Firmly but politely, Hugh pushed the glass back toward Helene. "That's all right, Helene. Rhea will bring me some fresh tea."

As the dinner progressed—and to Jane it seemed endless—Helene chatted with Hugh, deliberately monopolizing him.

Jane caught herself feeling resentful toward the beautiful woman. But she told herself that she had no right to feel that way. After all, Hugh and Helene had known each other for ages. And she, Jane, was an outsider.

It came as a surprise, toward the end of the meal,

when Hugh turned to her and said, "I would like to speak to you, Jane, after we finish dinner. If that would be all right?"

"Of course," Jane said, wondering if she had done something wrong today and Hugh had decided not to keep her on at The Towers.

When Rhea had brought in the dessert, David said, "Be sure to have Jane tell you all about the games that she and Brandon were playing today. Katherine knows what they were up to, don't you, sister dear?"

Katherine gave David a wan smile and said, "Brandon seems to be in good hands with Miss Stewart."

"I'm sure he is," Helene said with a frosty edge to her voice. "Miss Stewart seems able to speak to him on his own level. But then, why not? She's practically a child herself."

Jane fought the desire to speak back to Helene, and Hugh did not appear to have noticed anything that the auburn-haired beauty had said.

Instead, he glanced at Jane and saw that she had nearly finished her dessert. "I'll meet you in my study, Jane, whenever you are finished."

Jane nodded as Hugh got to his feet and walked away from the table. Helene momentarily glared at her, then directed her attention toward David and Lorene. Katherine was speaking to Edgar Carrol, and so Jane wasn't particularly noticed as she got to her feet and walked away from the table. She was glad that dinner was over. It had been the longest meal that she could ever remember eating.

When Jane entered Hugh's study, he got to his feet and indicated a chair with his hand. "Please sit down, Jane. I would like to talk to you about my son."

Jane sat down and found that she was gazing into Hugh's dark, slightly amused eyes.

"I've been told that you and my son were using a stone to play ball today."

"It was just a game," Jane said quickly. "Brandon, as a matter of fact, was very good at it. That is, after he got the hang of catching the stone."

At the mention of Brandon's name, Hugh's face became slightly cloudy, and his eyes narrowed somewhat. But that expression was short-lived and he managed a slight smile. "I'm afraid the boy isn't used to playing games."

Jane had noticed that Hugh Hammett rarely used Brandon's name. It was as though the child were a stranger—and it made her heart ache.

"He did very well," she said quickly. "And I think the fresh air did him good. It can't be too healthy for Brandon staying in his room all the time."

"I'm responsible for that," Hugh said. "After what happened to Mother, I want to know where he is at all times. And I feel that he couldn't get into too much trouble being confined to his room."

Jane could tell that Hugh was convinced his son was responsible for the accident in the east wing. Yet she just couldn't bring herself to believe that

Brandon was capable of pushing someone in a wheelchair down the stairs. Especially if that someone was his own grandmother.

Then Hugh smiled at her and said, "Anyway, I want to tell you that I'm very pleased that you came to The Towers to work. I just hope that you won't be discouraged and leave. We've had several other people here in the past to look after Brandon, but none of them lasted too long."

Before Jane could ask why that had been so, Helene appeared at the door. She smiled at Hugh in an enticing way and said, "Don't you think I deserve equal time, Hugh? I really have something important to discuss with you. Surely you and Miss Stewart are finished by this time."

He said, "Of course, Helene. Jane and I were just finishing our conversation. If you have any problems with my son, please feel free to contact me at once, Jane."

With that Hugh walked over to Helene, who placed a hand on his muscular arm as she led him away from the study.

Jane just shrugged and got to her feet, telling herself she really should get back to Brandon.

When she got upstairs, she saw Edgar Carrol standing outside Dorothea Hammett's room. He must have sensed that he was being watched because he looked at Jane and then pivoted quickly and walked to his room.

Jane walked briskly down the corridor wondering why Mr. Carrol had acted so strangely. She saw that the door to Dorothea's room was opened slightly and she pushed it wide and walked in.

Hugh's mother was propped up in bed and her eyes were open. When she saw Jane, she quickly shut them, as though she wanted to pretend that she had been sleeping. Jane walked over to Dorothea's bed and stood there for a moment.

She didn't know where she got the boldness to speak, but she did. "Mrs. Hammett, I'm Jane Stewart. Your son has hired me to look after Brandon. I don't for a minute believe that the boy had anything to do with your accident. But I must warn you not to drink any milk that is brought to you. I have reason to believe that something might be put in it."

Jane happened to glance down and saw that the glass of milk Rhea had brought in was half hidden beneath the bed. Jane reached down and took the glass and went to the bathroom where she drained the contents. Then she brought the emptied glass back and put it on the tray that was near Dorothea's bed.

Turning to go, Jane took one final look at Dorothea and she saw a faint smile on the old woman's lips. It was a smile that told her Dorothea had understood everything she had said.

Chapter Ten

Leaving Dorothea's room, Jane went to Brandon's. He had eaten his supper and was in his night clothes. When he saw Jane, he hurried over to her with the book of stories.

"Read it to me, please, Jane," Brandon said with an eager look in his bright eyes.

"Okay. But you hop into bed first, and then I will."

Brandon raced to his bed and leaped in. He looked so small and vulnerable that a slight lump formed in Jane's throat as she read to him.

At breakfast the next morning Helene Kannon did not appear, and the other residents of the house ate a quick meal and went about their various ways. Hugh Hammett had apparently eaten an early breakfast and was at work in his study.

Jane had a second cup of coffee as she sat alone in the vast dining room. Reba came in while she was sitting there to gather up the dishes.

"Brandon was all dressed and ready for his breakfast this morning," she said in a cheerful way. "You must be doing something right. I've never seen him this way before. Not recently. He was asking about you and when you would be coming to see him."

Jane was pleased by Reba's words.

"As soon as I finish my coffee, I'll go up. Thanks, Reba."

"He really is a well-behaved little boy," Reba chatted on. "And he ate everything on his plate."

"I'm glad I had a good breakfast so that I'll have the energy to keep up with him today," Jane said. "Tell me, Reba, do you take Dorothea her meals sometimes?"

Reba quickly shook her head. "Only Rhea. I guess it just sort of happened that I would mostly bring Brandon his meals and Rhea would take care of Miss Dorothea."

Jane finished her coffee and left the dining room. As she was walking toward the stairs, she met Katherine. Hugh's sister was as formal as ever, but she did pause for a moment to speak to Jane.

"We didn't have much of a chance to speak at breakfast. Hugh has turned over the running of the house to me since Mother became ill. It's such a vast place that it does require a lot of attention."

"I would imagine."

"That's why I left so abruptly at breakfast, to get on with my work. And how is your work going with Brandon?"

There was no way of telling if Katherine was seriously interested in Brandon or just being polite. Katherine rarely smiled and she appeared always to be wearing a mask.

"I think I'm making progress with him. Reba told me at breakfast that Brandon was up and dressed and wanted to see me."

Katherine nodded. "I wouldn't expect too much at first, Miss Stewart. Brandon is a strange child. He always has been. You never really know what he is thinking or what he will do."

The words were chilling coming from Katherine and Jane for a moment lost the enthusiasm she had experienced earlier. Then she quickly shook off her depression and smiled at Hugh's sister.

"People do change, you know. And I have a feeling that Brandon and I will become very close friends."

Katherine said, "Personally, I hope that you are right. Just don't be too disappointed if that doesn't come to pass."

Katherine excused herself and Jane went upstairs. But before going into Brandon's room, she decided to look in on Dorothea. The old woman was lying just as she had last night, propped up with pillows and practically in the same position. And she was awake. Jane walked over to her bed and looked down at the woman.

"I hope you are feeling much better today, Mrs. Hammett. I know that you don't speak, but maybe you can understand what I'm saying. Brandon and I went outdoors yesterday and played. At first, he was unsure of himself, but I encouraged him, and he really seemed to enjoy playing catch with a stone we found."

Dorothea's face remained expressionless, yet Jane sensed that she was getting through to her. She had grown fond of the woman, even though she barely knew her.

"I just thought you might want to hear about your grandson. He's really a fine little boy and I think we're going to get along just wonderfully. I'd better be going now. Brandon probably wants me to read to him some more. We're into a marvelous book of stories at the moment."

Jane turned and walked to the door. Before she went into the corridor, she couldn't help but turn and look at Dorothea. She couldn't be certain, but she thought she saw another faint smile on the elderly woman's face.

Brandon's door was open and Jane found him sitting on the floor surrounded by the miniature ships.

When Brandon saw Jane, he started to get to his feet. "Are you going to read to me some more, Jane?"

"In a little while," she said. "Why don't you show me all these ships first. We have plenty of time to get back to the book."

"Do you really want to look at them?"

"Of course, I do," Jane said with a faint chuckle. "Tell me about each and every one of them."

Jane squatted on the floor next to Brandon as he began to explain, in detail, all about each ship. As he talked, his eyes grew wide with excitement and Jane was amazed at his knowledge of these vessels.

Very abruptly, though, he stopped speaking. Jane realized that he was staring at something behind her.

She turned her head to see Hugh Hammett standing in the doorway. His face was a mixture of fatherly affection and concern.

"Well, I haven't seen you play with those things in a long time," Hugh said as he entered the room.

But now Brandon was sitting stiffly, looking down at the floor.

"Your son was telling me all about his models," Jane said quickly so that the boy's tension would not be noticed. "We've been having a very interesting time."

"Yes, Brandon is quite an expert on his ships," Hugh said. The tone of his voice indicated that he was aware of the change in the atmosphere. "Well, I won't be staying. I just was passing by and thought I would check in on you, Jane. If you have any questions that Brandon can't answer, I'll be more than willing to speak to you." Then he left.

After Hugh had gone, Brandon just went on talking about the ships as though his father had not been in the room. But Jane could not forget the fatherly look on Hugh's face. He had truly wanted to be with his son.

At lunchtime Reba brought some hot soup and sandwiches, and then Jane read some more to Brandon. When he grew sleepy, she took him to his bed for a nap and decided that she would have a look at the house while he slept.

Walking down the corridor, Jane once again realized how quiet this huge, sprawling mansion could be.

As she passed Dorothea's room, she was tempted to stop and look in on her but thought that perhaps she, like her grandson, was taking a nap. Then Jane found herself thinking about the event that had shaken both of them so much—the accident that had occurred in the east wing. Jane couldn't help but wonder what had actually taken place in there.

And suddenly she found that she had wandered beyond the first staircase and into the east wing. Here it was dark and shadowy, and she had the feeling that it would soon be dank and musty, like some cellar that had long been unused.

Jane was tempted to turn around and go back the way she had come, yet she felt compelled to go on.

She was standing at the head of the east-wing staircase. This must have been where the accident had occurred. She tried to imagine both Dorothea and Brandon here, with Brandon behind the wheelchair. Even in her wildest imagining, Jane could not believe that Brandon had pushed his grandmother down the stairs. Yet what did she really know of the little boy? So far, since she had been at The Towers, she had hardly heard anything that wasn't negative about him.

A slight shiver ran down Jane's spine. She felt as though someone were watching her. She looked around, but she saw nobody. Then she moved away from the stairs and came to a room with an open door.

Jane walked into the room and gazed around. Across from her there was another door that seemed to be beckoning her. As long as she had come this far, she felt that she should find out all she could about the east wing.

Jane slowly began to cross the carpeted floor and paused. She turned around to stare behind her with that overwhelming feeling that she was being followed. Again she saw nobody.

When she came to the door, Jane reached out and opened it. She found that it led to a small room with a balcony that had barely enough floor space to stand on. Curious, Jane stepped out to the balcony. She stood there for a moment or two and gazed down at the concrete drive below.

For an instant she felt dizzy, but that was just because the railing on the balcony was so low. Jane took a step backward, and that was when she heard the door close behind her.

Turning around, Jane reached out and took hold of the doorknob. She tried to turn it. It wouldn't budge. Apparently, after being unused for so long, the door must have gotten stuck. Jane began to pound on it, slowly at first, and then with a burst of energy that had a great deal of nervousness in it.

She had drawn her fist back once again to pound when the door suddenly opened.

"Why, Miss Stewart," came the mocking tone of David Hammett's voice. "What are you doing out there?"

Jane quickly explained to David what had happened to her, and she saw a faint, smug smile touch his lips.

"You really shouldn't be walking around in the east wing alone," he said. "The place isn't used anymore. Just about anything might happen to you here."

Jane stared at David and deep inside she wondered if he had been the person who had followed her into the east wing, the person who had deliberately shut the balcony door behind her.

Chapter Eleven

Jane managed to get away from David Hammett as quickly as possible and hurried back down the corridor and out of the east wing. She went directly to her room and closed the door behind her. Alone, in the safety of her bedroom, she thought about what had just happened to her.

Had it been David Hammett who had followed her into the east wing? Jane had felt the presence of someone else when she had been in that part of the house. David had said that he had heard someone pounding on the door and had hurried to her rescue. That may or may not have been the truth.

But if it wasn't David, then who else could it have been? The first person who came to mind was Helene Kannon. Jane and Helene certainly hadn't struck up the greatest friendship in the world since she had arrived at the house. Jane could certainly visualize the auburn-haired beauty closing the door behind her and doing it with a certain amount of satisfaction.

After Helene there were any number of people in the mansion who might have done it—starting with the head of the house, Hugh Hammett himself. It seemed ungrateful of her to harbor such thoughts about the man who had hired her to work here, but

Jane knew so very little about Hugh, or for that matter, anyone else in the house.

She walked to the window and gazed out at the scenery below, but she saw nothing since she was so absorbed in her thinking. Had it been Edgar Carrol who had followed her down the corridor and waited until she had stepped out on the balcony and then slammed the door shut behind her? Or had it been Lorene? Or Rhea? Maybe even Katherine?

With a sigh, Jane turned from the window. Maybe it had been an accident. What motive would there be for someone to do such a thing to her? And then Jane remembered the first night she had come to The Towers, the night she had gone into Brandon's room. Someone had been there. Someone had meant to harm her that night.

No, Jane decided, it hadn't been an accident, her being locked out on the balcony in the east wing. Someone had done it deliberately.

In the next few days Jane slowly began to forget her mishaps in Brandon's dark room and in the east wing. She was busy with Brandon and that kept her from thinking about her own problems, and there was no other incident that caused her to wonder about her safety.

She took Brandon outside during the day for a few hours and the pale, wan look on his features began to fade. He sometimes found it difficult to play since he was such a serious little boy. But Jane coaxed him and joked with him and egged him on to be himself and relax.

Brandon was particularly fond of playing catch and he found various stones and sticks to use. Jane made a mental note that when she got to Mountain Pass, she would find them a good ball to play with. And maybe she'd pick up a few additional toys.

She found other books to read to Brandon and he was an eager listener. Jane enjoyed the reading times in his room or in the garden where they sprawled on the grass under a tree. Yet Brandon never seemed to relax totally. There was always a tenseness about him. He was like some alert animal that was ready to bolt and run at a strange sound or a harsh word.

Jane was becoming very attached to the little boy. And she found that her thoughts occasionally strayed to Brandon's father. The few times she saw Hugh, at meals mostly, he was very charming. And sometimes he was quite witty. There were moments she longed to be around him more, to find out what his likes were, what he thought about things. Then she would remember Helene. And she would tell herself she knew better than to pursue this avenue of thought.

One evening Jane had been on the front porch, looking up at the stars in the clear, cloudless sky, and Hugh had come to her side.

"It's really something, isn't it?" he had said as he stood in the shadows.

"Yes, it certainly is. It wouldn't take much for me to fall in love with Utah," Jane said absently.

"I'm pleased that you like our state," Hugh said. "But then you have a lot of spectacular scenery in Colorado."

"Have you been there?" she asked.

"I travel a lot," Hugh said. "That is, I did until a while ago. After the accident, I decided to curtail a lot of my traveling. I want to keep an eye on Mother and on the boy."

Jane again noticed how Hugh deliberately avoided calling his son by his first name. Each time that happened, she wondered if it had always been the same way with Hugh. Had there ever been a time when he had frequently called his son Brandon?

"One of these days I'll have to take you and the boy out for a picnic," Hugh said. "That way you can really get a chance to enjoy our countryside."

"I'd like that."

"Very well. I'll hold you to your word," Hugh had said, and there was a touch of lightness in the tone of his voice.

Sitting under a tree with Brandon at her side and a book open on her lap, Jane thought about that night and how Hugh could be so changeable in his moods. Sometimes he could be quite lighthearted and attentive, and then, other times he seemed remote and withdrawn with a surly look on his handsome face.

"Quite a picture you two make," Hugh said, walking toward them. He looked very attractive and rugged in a buckskin jacket and a yellow shirt tucked into a pair of Levi's.

"I was reading to Brandon," Jane said needlessly.

She closed the book on her lap and felt Brandon grow tense at her side.

"It's such a beautiful day, I thought maybe the

three of us would go on that picnic I promised you," Hugh said.

Jane suddenly sprang to her feet and reached for Brandon's hand. "A picnic! That sounds wonderful. Doesn't it, Brandon?"

Brandon didn't say anything. He just looked down at his shoes. But Jane couldn't help but feel that he was as excited as she was about going.

"When do we go?" she asked.

Hugh laughed. It was a pleasant, good-natured laugh and it seemed to fit him better than the scowl he often wore on his face.

"Right now. Or in a few minutes. I have to get the Land Rover out. And the cook has fixed us a basket to take with us."

"We'll have to change," Jane said, glancing down at Brandon. "It won't take us very long."

"Good. I'll meet you in front of the house in a few minutes."

Not waiting, in case Hugh might change his mind, Jane took Brandon's hand and they both hurried toward the house.

"This will be fun," Jane said to Brandon as she opened the front door. "You like picnics, don't you?"

"Never been on one."

"Well, it's about time you were," Jane said in a lighthearted tone. "My brother and I used to go on them all the time. We would hike around the mountains and explore and do all kinds of interesting things."

As they neared the stairs, Helene Kannon met them.

"My, aren't we in a big hurry," she said frostily.

"Brandon and I are going on a picnic," Jane said, not allowing the cold tone of Helene's voice to spoil their enthusiasm.

"Just the two of you?"

Brandon spoke for the first time since they had entered the house. "My father is taking us. We're going to climb mountains and things."

Helene's eyebrow rose in a cynical arch. "I hope the three of you have a wonderful time," she said, but there was nothing in her voice that convinced Jane she was sincere.

"I think we will," Jane said.

Helene's eyes blazed with fury for an instant and then she smiled. "I'm sure that you will. Excuse me."

After Helene was gone, Jane and Brandon went upstairs. Jane took Brandon to his room and told him what to put on, and then she hurried to her room to change. She slipped on jeans and a T-shirt and pinned her hair back. When she looked in the mirror, she was satisfied with what she saw and left the room.

Brandon was just about ready, except for his shoes. Jane helped him finish with the laces.

When they left Brandon's room, they met Katherine, who was carrying a clipboard in one hand and a pen in the other.

"You two seem to be dressed for outdoor things," Katherine commented, and Jane felt Brandon's hand tighten in her own.

"Hugh is taking us on a picnic," Jane said, trying not to linger too long in the house.

"A picnic!" Katherine said in an imperial way. "You can't be serious. Not with Brandon along."

"Of course, with Brandon. It will do him a lot of good. And I'm sure he will enjoy himself."

"Have a good time," Katherine said with a slight tone of censure.

"Thank you," Jane said. "I think we will."

Brandon appeared glad when Katherine walked away. Then he and Jane hurried down the stairs. They saw Hugh standing at the bottom.

"If you both are ready, then we can leave," Hugh said. He appeared to be as excited as they were about going on the picnic.

Taking Jane's arm, Hugh led them outside to where the Land Rover was waiting. Brandon crawled into the backseat and Jane sat next to Hugh. Hugh glanced over his shoulder at Brandon before he drove away. Jane felt that he was checking on his young son the way any father would under the circumstances.

As they drove through the countryside, Jane and Hugh talked about various things and she found they had a great deal in common. Brandon did not say a word, only answering Jane when she spoke to him. Hugh never once spoke to Brandon, and his son did not venture to ask him anything or try to carry on a conversation.

By this time, Jane was getting used to the attitude of the two, even though it vexed her somewhat that they couldn't have a more relaxed relationship.

About an hour later, Hugh drove the car off the main road and onto a dusty, little-used byroad. The road, which had steep cliffs on one side, ran down until it reached a gently moving stream.

"How's this for the ideal picnic spot?" Hugh asked as he parked the car.

"Couldn't be more perfect," Jane said, opening her door and reaching for Brandon's hand.

Hugh opened the trunk of the car and brought out two blankets and a large picnic hamper. While he spread the blankets on the ground near the base of a cliff, Jane and Brandon walked over to the stream.

"Are you having a good time?" Jane asked and Brandon just nodded his head.

He still wasn't ready to meet his father even halfway.

The three of them walked along the bank of the stream and Hugh occasionally reached down and picked up a small stone and skimmed the surface of the water with it. Jane saw that Brandon was watching his father but made no effort to imitate his actions.

By the time they had finished their walk, Jane was hungry and helped Hugh with the hamper, which held fried chicken, a crisp salad, and some cheese and fruit. Even Brandon had an appetite.

When they had finished with the meal, Brandon got up and wandered away. Jane started to follow him, but Hugh put up a warning hand.

"Let him go. He needs to get away by himself."

"I suppose you're right. But I was worried that he might get lost. Brandon is not used to all this like any boy his age should be."

"Brandon is wise beyond his years," Hugh said in a cold, chilling tone of voice that made Jane stare at him with questioning eyes.

After that Jane lay back on one of the blankets. The sunlight was warm on her eyelids and she found herself becoming drowsy. Before she let herself drift off into a nap, she glanced around and saw that Hugh had gone off somewhere by himself. Jane was too comfortable and relaxed to think about that and she settled back on the blanket.

She didn't know how long she had slept or what had awakened her. But all at once she sat up, completely alert. There was a noise, a sort of rumbling sound, and Jane glanced up at the cliff that was nearby. A fine trickle of loose earth came filtering down toward her, and she instinctively jumped up from the blanket.

And not an instant too soon. A huge boulder came crashing down from the cliff and fell with an ear-splitting crunch on the place where she had been lying only a moment before.

Chapter Twelve

Jane stood there staring at the boulder that might have been fatal to her if she hadn't awakened and acted so quickly.

From somewhere behind her she heard Hugh call out, "Jane! Jane! Are you all right?"

She pivoted quickly to see him running toward her. Worry and concern were etched on his face. Suddenly, Hugh was standing next to her and his hands were clutching her shoulders.

"I'm all right," Jane said in a rather shaky tone of voice. "I wasn't hurt."

"That was close," Hugh said. "Just what happened? I was taking a walk when I heard a rumble and it sounded as though it came from this direction."

"After I lay down, I must have dozed off. Something awakened me and I saw some loose earth coming down from the cliff and I just got out of the way. It was a good thing I did. You can see what happened."

Hugh glanced over her shoulder. Even though he appeared to be concerned about her, there was a strange look in his eyes that made Jane feel uncomfortable. At that moment Brandon came bounding down the side of the cliff.

Hugh released his grip on Jane's shoulders and she was thankful. For he was beginning to hurt her. Now he stood perfectly still, staring at his young son.

"So it was you who did this," Hugh said in a deep, angry tone of voice. "I might have known."

Brandon stopped in his tracks and stared at his father, not saying a word. Jane quickly walked over to where Brandon was standing.

He looked up at her and said, "I didn't do that. You know I wouldn't hurt you."

"I believe you," Jane said, taking the little boy's hand. "Let's just not think about it. It was an accident. But as you can see, I'm perfectly all right."

As they walked toward Brandon's father, Jane could see the smoldering anger in Hugh's dark eyes. Whatever friendship had begun to blossom between the two was certainly gone now. Hugh appeared to be remote and almost cold when they got to him.

"Where were you?" Hugh demanded of his son.

Brandon didn't reply. He just stood there glaring at his father. The two were so much alike, Jane thought as she glanced from one to the other.

"Of course, I didn't really expect an answer," Hugh said. "You seem to be around whenever there are accidents."

"Hugh, please don't," Jane said.

Hugh's eyebrow rose in a cynical arch. "We won't discuss this any further. I believe it's time for us to go back. I think my son has had enough of the outdoors for today."

Brandon obediently followed alongside Jane. He was clutching her hand so tightly that it was almost hurtful to her. Hugh opened the doors to the Land rover and Brandon quickly got into the backseat.

Jane glanced at Hugh as he took his seat behind the steering wheel. She was about to say something to Hugh in defense of Brandon, but she knew this was not the right time or place to speak of that. And then she wondered where Hugh had been when the boulder had come crashing down the side of the cliff. He said he had been out walking, but he could very easily have been the one who had sent the rock down the cliff. She certainly felt that he was far stronger than his son and could have had time to run down the cliff after the boulder had been pushed down its side.

If Hugh had been the one who had done such a thing, Jane wondered why. There didn't appear to be any motive for such an action. Then she thought about the other girls who had held her job before she came. There must have been some reason they didn't stay at The Towers too long. Had similar things happened to the others?

They hardly said a word to each other on the return trip. Hugh was positively surly. Jane looked out the window at the passing scenery, but she was too preoccupied with her thoughts to really enjoy the beauty of the landscape.

She was thankful when she saw the high fence that guarded The Towers. What had started out to be such a pleasant day had ended on a sour note.

Hugh parked the Land Rover and opened the door for Jane and waited until Brandon was out of the car. Then he said, "I'm glad that you weren't harmed, Jane. Now I have work to do." He sounded rather brusque.

Jane took Brandon up to his room.

"You think I did that, don't you?" Brandon said, his eyes as hard as his father's.

"Of course, I don't," Jane said. "Why would you want to hurt me? It was just an accident. Try not to think about it anymore."

"But my father thinks I did it," Brandon said with despair.

Jane told him, "Let's just forget about all that now. We only have a few more stories in the red book. Do you want to hear them?"

Those words seemed to snap Brandon out of his dark mood, and a bright, eager smile touched the corners of his mouth.

Jane got the book and they sat on the floor, leaning their backs against the wall, as she began to read. She found that by concentrating on the book she was temporarily able to shut out any thoughts about the picnic. Once or twice she glanced down at Brandon and saw that he was listening intently to what she was reading.

When she had finished two stories and only one remained, she closed the book and said, "We'll save that last one for tonight, okay?"

Brandon agreed with her and Jane stayed with him for the better part of the afternoon, playing a board game that she had found in his closet. Then she instructed Brandon to take a bath and change his clothing while she did the same in her own room.

After Jane had changed for dinner, she sat before her mirror and absently ran a comb through her blond hair. She was thinking about the near-fatal accident that had happened that afternoon. She no longer could believe that it was an accident. Someone had deliberately pushed that boulder down from the top of the cliff, someone who wished to harm her, someone who did not want her to remain here at The Towers.

As Jane sat there, she suddenly felt that she heard a whisper in the house, a whisper of evil. And evil was reaching out to harm her, just as Dorothea had been harmed.

Jane was so deep in thought that she jumped when there was a rap at her door. When she opened the door, she saw Lorene Hammett standing there.

"I'm sorry. Am I disturbing you?" Lorene said in a nervous, apologetic voice.

"Of course, you aren't," Jane replied. "Is anything wrong?"

"Not really," Lorene said. "I mean, it's nothing that you could really put a finger on." She was twisting her hands nervously together. Something obviously was bothering the woman.

"Would you like to come in?" Jane said.

"I can't," Lorene said. "Just be careful while you are here in this house, Jane."

Before Lorene could say anything else, David came

out of their room and glowered at her. "Come along, Lorene, we'll be late for supper."

Lorene quickly hurried away from Jane and joined her husband. As they walked down the corridor, Lorene glanced back at Jane, a frightened look in her eyes.

Jane waited until they had gone downstairs. Then she looked in on Brandon and headed for the dining room herself. Lorene's warning echoed in her mind. How much did Lorene actually know about the danger that she was in? Jane wished she had had more time with David's wife before he had emerged from his room.

Casting a wary eye about the people who were seated at the table, Jane wondered which one of them was behind all that had happened to her since she had arrived at The Towers. It seemed such a long time ago that she had arrived, and yet it wasn't.

Taking a seat opposite Helene, who barely acknowledged her presence, Jane looked suddenly at Hugh and found that he was watching her.

Gone was the surly mood that had enshrouded him earlier that day. Now he smiled warmly at her. "You look very lovely tonight, Jane," he said, and Jane felt her face grow hot as she blushed.

Then she glanced across the table and saw the wide, green eyes of Helene narrow in jealousy.

Looking around her, Jane wondered again which person was responsible for the things that had happened to her since she had arrived at The Towers. Was it David Hammett? He was looking at her now in that haughty, lofty way that was so characteristic of him. Or maybe it was Lorene. Was she all that she seemed to be? Even though she appeared to be subservient to her husband, there was a strength there that Jane was suddenly aware of.

Dinner was pleasant, thanks mainly to the attentive actions of Hugh. Jane was once again surprised by his changeable ways. She wondered if she would ever get to know this moody, though charming man.

When coffee was served, Hugh excused himself and left the room. Jane found that she was left with Helene across the table from her.

"How was your little picnic, Miss Stewart?" Helene asked in an overly sweet tone.

"Quite enjoyable," Jane answered.

"You should be careful when you get into the wild country. Just about anything could happen to you."

Jane saw that there was a smug smile on Helene's face, and she read into it that Helene was fully aware of what had happened while she and Hugh and Brandon had been on their picnic.

Luckily, dinner was finally over and Jane decided to go to the library to find another book to read to Brandon and one for herself. The library was unoccupied when she entered and she walked over to the bookcase and began to study the titles.

As she stood there, she could hear two voices speaking across the corridor. The two people were apparently in the big den, which was hardly ever used by the residents of the house.

Jane didn't want to eavesdrop, but she could hardly

fail to hear what was being said. It took her a moment or two to figure out that the voices belonged to David and Lorene.

"But, David," Lorene was saying in a wavery tone, "those debts must be paid."

"Don't worry, I'll get the money."

"How? The allowance you receive isn't nearly enough to cover them."

"There'll be money coming in. Don't forget Mother's will. She can't last much longer."

Jane was thankful that the voices faded away then, as though David and Lorene had moved to another part of the den.

Jane took two books from the shelf and quickly walked out of the room. She hoped that she could get past the open door of the den without being seen. And she would have succeeded, had it not been for Hugh, who came walking toward her in the hallway.

"Jane, I see you've been in the library," he said in that familiar, deep voice, and Jane found a strange weakness taking over her knees and her insides.

"I thought I would find something for Brandon and myself," she said, hoping that her voice did not reveal the way her heart thudded.

Hugh's face momentarily clouded, but that quickly passed as he spoke again. "Sorry about the picnic today. I mean, about the way it ended. I'm glad that you weren't harmed."

Jane didn't reply for a moment. Then she said, "I enjoyed it too. All but the accident. I hope that we can do it again someday."

"I'm sure we will. After all, you will be here for some time. Won't you?"

"As long as Brandon needs me," replied Jane.

"Of course," Hugh said, and there was a curt politeness in his voice as he told her good night.

Jane walked past Hugh and resisted the impulse to glance back over her shoulder. When she neared the staircase, Reba was coming toward her.

It was good to see a friendly face and Reba was all smiles. "Brandon is in bed and he won't go to sleep until you finish reading a story for him."

"I'm on my way," Jane said. And then a thought came to her. "Reba, was Miss Kannon at the house when Dorothea had her accident?"

Reba thought for a moment, then said, "Yes, she was. But then she comes and goes all the time."

Jane thanked the maid, then went upstairs. When she got to the second floor, she saw that only a few lights were burning, and the corridor was dark and forbidding. As she headed toward the boy's room, she saw Edgar Carrol standing in the shadows, his eyes watching her every move.

Chapter Thirteen

Jane stayed with Brandon until he fell asleep. He looked so innocent and helpless that she just couldn't believe he was capable of hurting anybody.

After a few minutes, she got up and left the bedroom. She glanced around to see if Edgar Carrol was still in the corridor, but he was nowhere to be seen. Idly, Jane wondered what the old man had been up to, skulking around the corridor in that manner. She was tempted to go into Dorothea's room and see if she was all right. And that temptation got the better of her.

But she hesitated a moment before going in. Then just as she reached for the doorknob, the door opened. Hugh Hammett was standing there.

There was a surprised but pleasant look on his face as he said, "Aren't you in the wrong room?"

Jane felt a flush of prickly embarrassment spread through her cheeks. "I was just going to check on your mother. To see how she was doing."

Hugh glanced over his shoulder and said, "She's asleep. Would you care to see her?"

"No. I was just worried about her," Jane said and then regretted that she had spoken those words.

A curious eyebrow darted up on Hugh's ruggedly

handsome face. "Worried about her? Do you have a reason to be?"

"It's just that she seems so helpless in there and I check on her from time to time to see how she's doing. Maybe I shouldn't be doing that."

Hugh smiled at her. "Don't apologize. I think what you are doing is very commendable. But now that Mother is asleep, I was about to take a walk around the gardens. Would you be interested?"

Jane knew that she wasn't tired and a walk might do her good. "Yes, I would like that. I'll get a sweater and be right with you."

Hugh was waiting outside Dorothea's room when Jane emerged with a sweater draped around her shoulders. She didn't know if she would need one, but she wasn't accustomed to the weather in Utah at night.

As they walked down the stairs, Jane sensed that inquisitive eyes were following their every move and she got an uncomfortable feeling in the pit of her stomach. It was with a sigh of relief that she faced the darkness of the evening outside of The Towers.

"It's a beautiful night," Jane said as she and Hugh casually strolled away from the house.

"Slightly different from Colorado, I imagine," he said.

"Not that much, really," said Jane. "But Utah is a very interesting state."

Hugh didn't reply but kept on walking, as though he were lost in his thoughts. Jane happened to glance back at the house and she thought she saw a curtain quickly close at a downstairs window, as though someone had been watching them. She wondered if that person was Helene Kannon. Then Jane dismissed that thought from her mind and just enjoyed being with Hugh and watching the beauty of the evening.

Finally, he said, "I guess I was a little hard on my son today. So tomorrow I plan to make it up to both him and you."

Jane didn't say anything. She was waiting for Hugh to continue.

"How about taking a drive tomorrow? Just the three of us. I'd like to give my son a second chance. You see, we just haven't seen enough of each other lately. Ever since the accident, I haven't had much to do with the boy."

"That would be wonderful," Jane said. "Brandon will enjoy the ride, and I know I certainly am looking forward to it."

"Good, then it's settled. I think I can spare that much time with my son. Although I'm not sure that he will appreciate it."

The words were so harsh and condemning that Jane suddenly felt she was walking with a total stranger.

"Who is Edgar Carrol?" Jane suddenly asked in an effort to change the subject.

"Edgar? He was my father's best friend. They grew up together as boys. But he's not an easy person to get to know. He never cared much for anyone but my father and myself. From what I've been told, he just tolerated Mother when my father married. Yet Mother invited him here before her accident."

"What a strange man."

"He's changing," Hugh said. "He seemed very upset over Mother's accident. He sort of hovers around her. Originally, he just came for a brief visit, but it's turned out to be a much longer stay. Not that I mind. There is plenty of room in The Towers for everyone."

Jane wondered about Edgar Carrol as they retraced their steps to the house. Had he truly changed his attitude toward Dorothea, or had he perhaps been responsible for her accident?

By the time they reached the mansion, Jane found that she was yawning and ready to go to her room. Hugh said good night when they went inside and Jane hurried up the stairs. She remembered how Edgar Carrol had looked earlier when she had gone to Brandon's room. And he had been outside Dorothea's room that other time. What did he really want at The Towers?

There was another question that puzzled her. What connection did she, Jane, have with the accident in the east wing? She had no proof of anything—just a strong hunch that whoever had done such a terrible thing to Hugh's mother was now trying to harm her. But why? Why?

Unable to find answers, Jane told herself to relax. She read a little from the book she had taken from the library for herself. Then she tried to fall asleep. But it took her a long while despite her recent tiredness.

The next morning, after she dressed, Jane hurried over to Brandon's room and helped him with his clothing. She made certain that he looked particularly neat today so that his father would find no fault with him.

Jane found when she entered the dining room that she had obviously overslept. The only person at the table was Edgar Carrol, busily attacking a huge stack of waffles.

"You're late," he muttered as Jane grabbed a glass of orange juice and a slice of toast from the sideboard. She was too excited about the coming drive with Hugh to be really hungry.

"I overslept," she said as she took a seat opposite the rather surly man.

"That boy too much for you?" Edgar Carrol said, looking over his fork at Jane.

"You mean Brandon? Of course not," Jane replied and took a sip of her orange juice. "We're getting along just fine. He's really a great little boy."

Edgar Carrol made a sound with his mouth and then took a gulp of coffee. "You would find that statement very debatable around here."

Jane put down her glass and looked squarely at the older man. "I guess I would have to defend Brandon," she said. "From all I've seen of him, he has been well-behaved and sensitive."

Edgar Carrol's mouth twisted in a mocking grin.

"You're too new around here to be making any kind of judgment. We all know what Brandon is really like. All you have to do is go into Dorothea's room to see his handiwork."

She could not speak for a moment. She just stared at the man as he calmly went back to his food.

"You don't know that it was Brandon who pushed that wheelchair down the stairs," Jane finally said with more boldness than she felt.

"Who else could it have been?" said Edgar as he reached for his coffee. "Don't tell me you believe that someone besides Brandon pushed that wheelchair? That's totally without foundation."

"Were you there in the east wing when it happened?" Jane asked.

Edgar Carrol suddenly glared at her. "Of course, I wasn't."

"Then you don't really know that it was Brandon. Nobody actually saw him push Dorothea down the stairs."

"Young woman," Edgar Carrol said in a menacing voice, "you are treading on dangerous ground. Excuse me, please."

With those words Edgar Carrol got to his feet, wadded his napkin, and tossed it on the table. Then he walked briskly out of the dining room.

Jane didn't care if she had upset the man or not. Right now she was just angry that everyone in the house seemed to be taking sides against Brandon. She felt that, besides Reba and Raymond, she was his only champion. Perhaps that was dangerous and foolish, but she did not think Brandon was the little monster that everyone believed him to be.

Jane finished her toast and she too left the dining room. When she got to Brandon's bedroom, he was standing by the window looking outside. He turned to gaze at Jane as she walked toward him. There was a look of anticipation on his face that hadn't been there before.

"While we're waiting for your father, do you want me to read a little bit to you, Brandon?"

Naturally, Brandon was eager for that and he hurried over to the nightstand to get the new book. Jane had just turned a page when Hugh Hammett appeared at the door. He looked very handsome standing there and Jane felt that same uneasiness in the pit of her stomach that seemed to appear lately whenever she was around him.

"Well, everyone looks eager and ready to go," Hugh said.

"We are, aren't we, Brandon?" Jane said as she took Brandon's hand.

The boy didn't look at his father, but he nodded his head in an appealing way. Jane looked at Hugh and thought she saw the faint glimmer of a smile on his face.

As they left the house, Jane felt the presence of hostile eyes following them. She was tempted to turn around and look but kept walking straight ahead.

The ride ended up in Mountain Pass. Jane had time to look at the quaint, appealing little town as Hugh drove slowly down its main streets. He pointed out various businesses to Jane and made humorous comments about each one and also was, at the same time, complimentary, so that he didn't sound totally cynical.

It was getting close to twelve o'clock and Hugh glanced at his watch and said, "I'm all for going to a fast-food place and getting some hot dogs and taking them to the park. How does that sound?"

"Just great," said Jane as she glanced at Brandon, who appeared to like the idea too. "And lots of crunchy fries and a fattening shake."

Hugh laughed. It was the first time Jane had ever heard Hugh totally abandon himself to an honest, hearty laugh and she found it very agreeable. So the lord and master of The Towers could be human, after all.

When they had driven through the exit of the fast-food establishment, Hugh made a quick turn and directed the car to the outskirts of Mountain Pass. Here he gently touched the brake as they neared a grassy, almost deserted park.

Hugh found a table and some wooden benches near the playground and they sat down to eat. Jane found that Hugh was quite eager to talk and she listened raptly, chewing on her hot dog and just enjoying the company of Hugh Hammett and his young son. Brandon ate two hot dogs and allowed Jane to wipe the mustard from his chin as he eyed the rides in the playground. He particularly seemed to be interested in the slide with its high steps and its gleaming, metal slope.

Jane sensed that Brandon wanted to go play and, after he had eaten, she said, "Why don't you go over and play on the slide with that other boy, Brandon? He looks about your age."

Brandon hesitated at first and Jane felt it was because he had had very little contact with children his own age. Then she talked to him for a moment or two and encouraged him some more.

After he had gone, Hugh said, "You certainly have a way with children. My son would never have done that for me."

Jane cocked her head to one side and said, "I think you underestimate yourself. I believe that you and Brandon could be really close friends."

"Do you honestly think so?"

"Of course."

"The boy doesn't like me," Hugh said. "Or haven't you noticed? I don't understand him. There is an element of trouble connected with my son. For some reason, bad things always seem to happen when he's around."

Jane was about to say that Hugh didn't really believe that when they heard a scream—and they both turned to see a little boy lying on the ground near the slide, holding on to his sides as though he had fallen. Jane's eyes shifted to the top of the slide where Brandon was standing, looking down at the fallen boy.

Leaping to his feet, Hugh glared at Jane and said, "What did I tell you? Wherever Brandon is, you can be certain there will be trouble."

Chapter Fourteen

"Don't accuse Brandon until you know the full truth," Jane said in a gruff voice that matched Hugh's. "It could have been an accident."

Hugh rushed toward the slide and Jane was at his heels. In her heart she prayed that the little boy who fell was not seriously injured and that Brandon had had nothing to do with his fall. By the time they reached the slide, the boy was sitting up and wiping his eyes with his hand.

"Are you all right?" Hugh said as he knelt beside the youngster.

The boy nodded his head as a woman rushed over. She obviously was the boy's mother.

"Oh, Jeremy," the woman said. "I've told you time and time again not to play around on the top of the slide. It was that other boy's turn. You shouldn't have pushed him away. That's why you lost your balance and fell."

Hugh looked at Jane and she tried not to show victory in her face. Then Hugh turned to the woman. "How do you know that your son fell? He might have been pushed."

The woman shook her head. "No, he wasn't pushed. I was watching and saw the whole thing.

Jeremy has done this sort of thing before. That other little boy was first to slide, but Jeremy shoved him away. It wasn't that boy's fault."

With that, the woman took Jeremy by the hand and led him away.

Hugh turned and glanced up at Brandon and then back at Jane. "What can I say?"

"That's all right," Jane said, putting Hugh at ease. "I'm glad that little boy wasn't hurt."

Hugh watched as Brandon went down the slide and then raced around to climb the steps again. Jane wished that Hugh would show more enthusiasm toward Brandon and give him some kind of encouragement. But she knew that it had taken a long time to create that chasm that existed between them and it wouldn't be bridged overnight.

When the pair got back to the table, Hugh said that he wanted to be alone for a while and wandered away. Jane watched him as he moved among the trees, his head slightly bent as though he were deeply in thought. Then she checked on Brandon, who never seemed to tire of the slide.

Now that Jane was alone, she had time to think about some things that had been bothering her. She thought about the milk that Rhea had brought Dorothea and the strange substance that she had slipped into the glass. But more than the substance she recalled the box that had the initials H.K. Those initials could only stand for Helene Kannon. But why would Helene be trying to drug Dorothea? Did she want the old woman out of the way so that she would be free to marry Hugh when he had claimed his inheritance? It sounded frightful, but it was a plan that Jane felt Helene Kannon was fully capable of devising.

But what of Hugh himself? Did he want his mother out of the way too? From what Jane had gotten to know of Hugh, he appeared to be a man who wanted to control things. There was little doubt in Jane's mind that Hugh was a strong, dominating person. Would he go so far as to get rid of his own mother in order to have The Towers totally under his control? Even though she was sitting in the sun, Jane felt a slight chill as she thought about Hugh.

But there were others in the house who might want Dorothea out of the way, for their own reasons. She knew that David and his wife had discussed finances and David certainly had made no bones about needing money.

Jane already knew about Edgar Carrol and his relationship with Dorothea's husband. Had he, for some twisted reason, blamed Dorothea for taking his friend away? And now that that friend was gone, was he taking steps to do away with her? It sounded implausible, yet Jane thought such things were possible.

And she knew she mustn't discount Katherine. Although she had seen so very little of Hugh's sister and hardly knew anything about her, Katherine was a strong, yet secretive person. Even as Jane thought about Hugh's sister, she could hardly remember what the woman looked like.

"Two pennies for your thoughts?" came a voice that brought her out of her reverie.

Jane looked around and saw Hugh standing next to her. "*Two* pennies?" she asked.

"Inflation."

They both laughed then, and Jane once again marveled at how Hugh changed when he smiled. There was a warmth about him that made her completely forget how dour and sullen he looked at other times.

"Nothing you would be interested in," Jane said, not really wanting to tell Hugh what her thoughts had been.

"How is my son doing?" Hugh asked and Jane quickly turned in alarm to find Brandon. She was relieved that he was still on the slide and appeared to be having a very enjoyable time.

"I think maybe you might have to end up buying him that slide to take home," Jane said in a lighthearted way.

Hugh looked at the slide and his son, and Jane saw the smile that had lighted up his face fade. "Maybe we'd better be going back to the house. I think the boy has had enough of the outdoors."

"Very well," Jane said somewhat reluctantly. She felt that even though Brandon had been playing for quite some time, his father had made no effort to show any interest in him or what he was doing. But that would come with time, Jane felt as she walked over to the slide.

"Time to go, Brandon," she said and she saw the

discouraged look on his face at those words. "But we'll do it another time. Okay?"

"Okay," Brandon said as he took one final slide and then hurried over to Jane.

He let her take his hand as they walked back to the car. Jane couldn't help but notice the way Brandon avoided looking at his father, while Hugh avoided speaking to or looking at his young son.

On the way back to the house, she managed to keep up a flow of conversation with Hugh. Brandon just sat quietly in the backseat and watched the passing scenery. It was at times like these that Jane wondered just what was going on in the boy's mind. And, shifting her eyes from Brandon to Hugh, she wondered the same thing about Brandon's father. He was such a moody person, she wondered if she would ever get to know the real Hugh Hammett. Fortunately, the times when he was in a deep, black mood were rare and seemed to be getting rarer.

"Are you having a good time today?" Hugh asked at one point.

"Very much so," replied Jane as she studied Hugh's ruggedly handsome face. "At least there hasn't been a boulder coming down the hillside."

At those words, she noticed a faint, mocking smile touch Hugh's lips. Then he changed the subject. "This must all seem very remote and dull to you."

"What?"

"All this," Hugh said as he made a sweeping gesture with one hand, indicating the passing scenery.

"Not a bit," was Jane's quick reply. "I'm not a big-city woman. I grew up in a small town. Although I would like to travel—even though I really haven't seen much of the world in my lifetime."

"Well, you are young," Hugh said in an amused tone of voice. "You will have a lot of time to travel. I'm surprised that you stayed this long at The Towers."

"What do you mean?"

"Just that the others didn't last more than half a week. Somehow The Towers or Brandon just didn't agree with them."

Jane shot a quick look toward the backseat, but Brandon was staring out the window and she hoped that he hadn't heard what his father had just said.

"Or you just might have not picked the right people," Jane said. "It might not have had anything to do with either the house or your son. They probably would have left any job they had, for one reason or another."

That mocking smile was again on Hugh's full, sensuous lips. But he said nothing and there was an uncomfortable silence between them that lasted for the remainder of the ride back to The Towers.

At the house Hugh let them both out and then drove the Land Rover away to park it in the garage. Jane took Brandon by the hand and walked inside the house.

Mrs. March met them and looked as solemn and unfriendly as ever. "How was your picnic?" she asked in a frosty tone of voice.

"Just wonderful," Jane replied. "Brandon had a great time on the slide. Didn't you, Brandon?"

Brandon was looking down at his shoes and he just nodded his head.

"You certainly couldn't tell by this child that he did," Mrs. March said. "He's just as quiet as he's ever been. Ever since what happened to poor Mrs. Hammett."

Jane ignored the woman and said, "Let's go to your room, Brandon. Then we can talk."

Banishing the cold look the housekeeper gave her, Jane walked past her with Brandon and up the stairs.

What a cold, insensitive woman she is, Jane couldn't help but think as they reached Brandon's room. No wonder the boy never spoke to anyone; he was always being put down.

Jane stayed with Brandon until he had settled down for his nap. When she was convinced that he was sound asleep, she went to her room and decided that she would rest a while before dinner. She had made up her mind that she would eat with Brandon tonight. Jane felt that the boy needed her presence to reassure him that evening.

Instead of going to sleep, Jane suddenly went down the hallway to Dorothea's room. She rapped lightly before going in to make certain that she would find the old woman alone.

Going up to Dorothea's bed, she saw that the woman's eyes were open. Reaching down, Jane felt beneath the covers that touched the floor until she found the glass and then she went to the bathroom and emptied the drugged milk.

When she came back, she smiled at Dorothea and said, "You are beginning to look better. I hope that someday you will trust me enough to speak to me." But today was not that day and Jane quietly left the room to return to her own.

That evening she stayed with Brandon and had her meal brought in by Reba. She and Brandon made a big thing out of eating together and she found that, alone, the boy began to open up to her and they had a very enjoyable time together.

It had almost become a ritual that Jane would wait until Brandon was snuggled into his bed, and then she would get the latest book out and read a story to him. He tried to remain awake until she had finished what she was reading, but often he would nod off to sleep. Then Jane would tuck the covers beneath his chin, leave the night light burning, and tiptoe out of his room.

This evening was no exception, and when Jane had finished reading, she decided to take a short stroll outside.

As she left the house, she felt the presence of someone and turned to see David Hammett coming toward her.

"Mind if I join you?" he asked in a noncommittal tone of voice.

"If you like."

"I do," he said and then quickened his step until he was next to her. "Well, Miss Stewart, you seem to be making remarkable progress with that nephew of mine. I suppose you are to be congratulated."

"Brandon isn't all that hard to get to know," Jane said smoothly.

"Isn't he? You would have to go a long way to convince a lot of people living in our house."

"Does that go for you too?"

David waited a beat and then said, "Maybe. I'm not convinced that Brandon isn't what everyone says he is."

Jane felt her hands clench at her sides. She was becoming tired of hearing all these terrible things about Brandon. But David suddenly switched the topic from Hugh's son to Dorothea.

"Right now he's not my concern. It's Mother. I don't know what's keeping her going. She really is getting frailer by the day."

Jane listened intently to David, even though she did not like the direction his conversation had taken.

"If she were gone, then all the money I was promised would come to me. And, believe me, Lorene and I could use it. But I guess some things just can't be rushed."

Jane almost felt sick to her stomach at the way David so coldheartedly spoke of his ailing mother. It was as though he were a vulture waiting for her to die. She quickly changed the subject and directed their walk back to the house.

As they neared the front of The Towers, Jane saw Lorene standing on the porch watching them. Even in the dim light cast by the weak overhead electrical fixture, she could see the distrustful look in Lorene's eyes.

"Well, my dear," David said to his wife, "you shouldn't be standing out in the night air. You might catch a chill."

Lorene took David's arm and together the two of them went inside the house. Jane waited for a moment or two, and then she entered the house.

It was quiet, and Jane got that awful feeling that watchful eyes were upon her as she climbed the stairs.

Instead of going to Brandon's room, she went to Dorothea's. For some reason the woman was on Jane's mind tonight. She even felt that Dorothea might be in danger.

Chapter Fifteen

Dorothea was asleep. Jane went softly to her bed and brought a chair over to be near her. Looking at the sleeping woman, Jane wondered why she had come into her room.

She had been summoned here to take care of Brandon, not Dorothea. And she probably was overstepping her bounds in coming boldly into this room. Yet Jane really felt that Brandon's problems were related to those of his grandmother.

It was impossible for Jane to believe that Brandon had any connection with what had happened to Dorothea. In the brief time that she had come to know the boy, she had found that there was no malice or wickedness in him. But could she possibly be deceived? There had been other girls who had come to The Towers to take care of Hugh's son, and they had all stayed only a brief time. Why? What or whom had driven them away?

Jane thought about the incident in Brandon's dark room and her close escape from the boulder—and she grew increasingly certain that similar things must have happened to the other girls who had come to take care of Brandon. Jane didn't think she was any braver than any of those others. Why, then, had she remained here at The Towers?

Was it just a stubborn streak that she had inherited from her father? She thought it probably was a combination of that and her feelings for Brandon. He was just a little boy and he needed somebody on his side. Jane had always felt sorry for the underdog, and Brandon was just that.

Or was there yet another reason for her determination to remain here at the house? She couldn't deny the fact that she was finding herself attracted to Hugh Hammett. It wasn't something that she had planned on. And she was fully aware that this was a dangerous position for her to be in. For Helene Kannon was certainly a very deadly adversary, and a very beautiful one.

With a sigh, Jane still continued to look at Dorothea. She wondered if the best thing, after all, might be for her to pack up her things and leave The Towers and return to Colorado.

It was just a passing thought and Jane knew in her heart that she couldn't abandon Hugh's son and also Hugh's mother. Jane squared her shoulders with new resolution. She would not give up; she would not go running back to Colorado. She had been hired to do a job and she wouldn't leave until she felt Brandon no longer needed her.

Jane was so caught up in her thoughts that she didn't hear Katherine enter the room behind her.

"Why are you here?" Katherine asked in a quiet voice.

Jane felt uneasy under Katherine's sharp eyes. "I sometimes come in and check on Mrs. Hammett. Just to see if she needs anything."

Katherine made a faint sound and then said, "As you can see, Mother is not capable of asking for any help. She hasn't spoken a word since the accident."

Jane remained seated since Katherine had not ordered her out of the room. From the look on Katherine's face, Jane assumed that she really did not care one way or the other if Jane were in the bedroom.

"Has the doctor given you any hope that this will pass?"

Katherine slowly moved her head from side to side. "It's all up to Mother. But I don't think she wants to get well. All of her spirit is gone. She's just an old woman. In a way, it might be a blessing if she died."

Jane thought those were cruel words. But she had almost grown accustomed to hearing such things spoken at The Towers. She waited, wondering if Katherine would go on speaking. Perhaps she would get to know Hugh's sister a little better.

"I've never married, you know. After Father died, Mother was totally incapable of managing the house and Father's business interests. So I took over. To tell the truth, I've been doing that for years. Mother was never a very practical person; she was a dreamer. Never a very assertive woman. Then Hugh gradually took over the financial interests and left The Towers in my hands."

This was the most that Katherine had ever said to Jane, and she was eager to learn more about this reserved and remote sister of Hugh Hammett's.

"To tell the truth, I'm becoming a little tired of it all. After all, I'm not getting any younger. Maybe it would be best for all of us if Mother just let go."

"Why haven't you left the house?" Jane said. "Surely, Hugh could find someone to manage it. Mrs. March seems quite capable."

Katherine didn't seem to have heard Jane. She stood there looking down at her mother. "I was not one of Mother's favorites. She always preferred Hugh or David to me. Even though I did all I could to please her."

"I'm sure that your mother loved you."

"How can you say that? You don't know anything. You just came here."

It was a curt, cutting remark, but Jane felt that perhaps she had overstepped herself. So she did not resent what Katherine had said.

"That's true. I guess I was thinking about my own family. And how much my mother loves me."

"Then you are very lucky," Katherine said in a frosty tone of voice. "How are things going with you and Brandon?"

Jane was thankful that Katherine had changed the subject.

"Very well. Brandon seems to like me and, in time, I think he'll open up to me. I have a feeling that Brandon is hiding some secret. When the right time comes, he'll tell me."

Katherine had switched her attention from the woman in the bed to Jane. There was a glimmer of interest in her face.

"Maybe you will be good for Brandon. But I wouldn't count on him opening up to you. Others before you have tried. Brandon is a very strange little boy. And a very threatening one."

"Threatening? In what way?"

Katherine's hands were tightly clenched. "After all, he was with Mother in the east wing when it happened. Doesn't that tell you something?"

"I'll admit it does look bad for him. But can you be sure that it was Brandon who caused the fall?"

Katherine turned to Jane, her face a mask. There was not one bit of emotion showing on her stern features.

"You aren't thinking that it was somebody else who did this to Mother? That's not possible."

"Why not? After all the time I've spent with Brandon, I just can't believe that he would be capable of doing such a terrible thing."

"Then you don't know the real Brandon. After all, you've spent just a brief time with him. He can be very clever and deceiving."

"That's a side of Brandon I've yet to see," Jane said.

"I hope you never do."

These words were spoken so coldly that a quick chill raced down Jane's neck. Had she been blinded by Brandon's seemingly innocent behavior? Was he really the terrible person that everyone in the house seemed to believe him to be?

No, she thought. She was right. She just didn't blame Brandon for the accident. She would never be convinced that he was capable of such an act.

"I have things to do," Katherine said. "You can stay here if you wish. But I think it's just useless trying to communicate with Mother. She's beyond all that."

Katherine pivoted sharply and walked out of Dorothea's bedroom. Jane watched her leave and then turned her attention back to Dorothea. The woman's eyes were wide open now and they were staring at her.

Jane hoped that she hadn't heard a word that had been spoken between herself and Katherine. Perhaps Dorothea had just awakened.

"Brandon and his father and I went into Mountain Pass today," Jane said quickly. "We had a very nice time, although I forgot to get him some new toys as I'd planned to. Brandon played on the slide and he seemed to be enjoying himself. I thought that you would like to know that."

There was no indication that her words were getting through to the old woman.

"I hope you don't mind my coming in like this," Jane went on. "It's just that I thought you might like to have some company. My name is Jane Stewart and your son has hired me to look after Brandon, in case I forgot to tell you that already. Hugh knows my brother and that's why he hired me for the job."

It seemed so futile, her talking to Dorothea. It

was like a one-way conversation with Jane doing all the talking and not getting even the slightest acknowledgement from the woman in the bed.

Jane began to tell Dorothea all about herself, her parents, and where she lived. She didn't know why she was doing this, but she felt compelled to do it—as though it were some form of therapy and perhaps, in some way, Dorothea might respond.

That response never came and, finally, Jane said, "I'd better go check on Brandon. He really enjoys my reading to him before he goes to sleep."

Walking out of the room, Jane paused at the door to look back. Dorothea was still watching her and her face was expressionless. Perhaps Katherine had been right. Perhaps it was hopeless to try and get through to the woman. Still, Jane thought, it doesn't do any harm to try.

When Jane got to Brandon's room, she instantly felt there was something wrong. Brandon was in bed with the covers pulled up to his chin. His eyes were wide open.

"Brandon? Are you all right?" Jane asked as she crossed the room to the bed.

Brandon just lay there, looking across the room at something. Jane followed his gaze and saw what he was looking at. One of his prize ships lay on the floor, totally demolished.

Jane picked up the pieces. It looked as though some vicious hands had deliberately mangled the ship and then tossed it to the floor.

"How did this happen?" Jane asked as she came

back to the bed. "You didn't do this, did you, Brandon?"

Brandon slowly moved his head from side to side. There was a look of terror in his eyes and Jane felt that he was beginning to withdraw into the same state she had first found him in.

"I believe you," Jane said, for she actually did. She knew how much Brandon loved those small ships and she knew that he would do nothing to harm them.

"Can you tell me who did that? Who was in the room with you, Brandon?"

Brandon didn't reply. He just lay there with that frightened look in his eyes. Jane knew she had to do something quickly.

She put the remains of the vessel in the closet and quickly shut the door. Then she came back to Brandon.

"We'll just get you another one of those. And we'll build it together. How will that be?" Jane asked, and she saw the terror begin to fade from Brandon's eyes.

Now that the ship was out of sight, he seemed to be responding to her once again.

"Now that you're all tucked in, shall we continue with the book?"

"Yes, Jane, read to me," Brandon said in a pleading voice.

Jane reached out and gently brushed a lock of his hair away from his eyes and then reached for the book on the nightstand.

As she began to read, she occasionally glanced at

the young boy and saw that the fright in his eyes was continuing to fade away.

Jane tried to keep her mind on the story but found it difficult to do. She just couldn't believe that anyone would be so cruel as to wreck one of Brandon's ships. Who was this person who was doing such terrible things in this house? She meant to find out.

It took a good hour of reading until Brandon finally went to sleep again. Jane sat by his side longer than she normally would, just to make certain that Brandon didn't wake up again and find himself alone.

When she was convinced that he was asleep, soundly and deeply, she walked over to the closet. She glanced down at the ship and a deep anger welled up inside her at the person who had been so cruel. Then she glanced back at Brandon and walked quickly out of the room.

Chapter Sixteen

Jane left Brandon's door slightly ajar as she entered the corridor. Instead of going to her own room, she went directly to Dorothea's. She felt compelled to speak to Hugh's mother, even though all of her talking might prove to be futile.

Dorothea was still lying in bed, in practically the same position she had been in earlier when Jane had been in the room. She was awake and her eyes followed the girl as she walked over to her bed.

Sitting on the chair by the bed, Jane looked intently at Dorothea. "I've got to talk to you, Dorothea. If you don't mind me calling you by your first name. Maybe you won't answer me, but I know you hear what I have to say. Just a little while ago, after I left your room, I went to Brandon's. A terrible thing had happened there.

"One of Brandon's ships was smashed. Totally senseless work. I know that Brandon wouldn't do such a thing. He loves those ships that his father bought him. I think it was someone in the house who did this thing. And I aim to find out who that person is."

All the time Jane was speaking to Dorothea, she

kept watching her for some sort of reaction. She did notice that Dorothea's eyes widened somewhat as she mentioned Brandon's name. Jane did not know whether it was concern for the little boy or a memory that came to her about what had happened in the east wing.

All at once Jane heard voices in the corridor, and she turned to see Rhea standing before the open door talking to Hugh. She could not hear what they were saying, but Hugh reached out and took the tray from the maid's hands. He touched the glass of milk and moved it slightly on the tray before he came into the room.

"Ah, Jane," he said as he walked toward the bed. "You and Mother having a little visit? I'm afraid your conversation will be a little one-sided."

"We're getting along just fine," Jane replied with more confidence than she actually felt.

"She's looking better," Hugh said. "More alert than I've seen her look in months. I don't suppose that would have anything to do with you. You seem to have a way of bring people out of their shells. However, in Mother's case, I think it is almost hopeless."

Jane didn't like the idea of Hugh speaking as though Dorothea couldn't hear him. Even if Dorothea chose not to speak, that did not mean that she didn't hear and understand what was being said around her.

"Nothing is hopeless," Jane said firmly.

"I admire your optimism," Hugh said as a crooked smile etched the edge of his full lips. "However misguided it might be."

Jane said nothing. She did not think that her optimism was misguided and she did not feel that Dorothea Hammett was a hopeless case. Like Brandon, all the woman needed was a little attention and concern. And if nobody else at The Towers could give that to Dorothea, she certainly would try.

"How are things with my son?" Hugh asked unexpectedly. "You have been in to see him, haven't you?"

Jane dismissed Hugh's tone of voice, since she had grown somewhat accustomed to his brusque and direct manner of speech.

"As a matter of fact, I just came from there. He's sleeping. I'll look in on him again before I go to bed."

"Nothing unusual about him or his room?"

Jane searched Hugh's face quickly. What did he know of the smashed ship? Had he been the one who had done that to his son?

She thought for a moment before she spoke. "As a matter of fact, somebody ruined one of Brandon's ships."

She saw Hugh's eyes narrow in a menacing way.

"What do you mean? What happened?"

"Just what I said. When I came into Brandon's room earlier, I found that one of the ships you had given him was smashed. It was a terrible thing to do to Brandon."

Hugh sniffed. "To Brandon? How do you know that he didn't do that himself? I never know what to make of that boy."

Jane began to feel indignation rising in her. It was all she could do to control that feeling. "It wasn't Brandon who did it. Hugh, your son loves those ships because you gave them to him. He wouldn't deliberately damage one of them."

"Wouldn't he?" Hugh said as he arched an eyebrow. "We'll talk about this in the morning. Now I'll leave Mother's tray with you. Maybe you might be able to coax her into eating something."

Jane took the tray that Hugh thrust toward her and stood there as he walked out of the bedroom. Surely Hugh couldn't believe that Brandon had smashed that ship. He had locked his son out of his heart for so long that he was incapable of believing anything good about Brandon.

Turning back to the bed, Jane placed the tray across Dorothea's lap and took the glass of milk away. "I'll get you some water. I think that will do you more good than this milk. Oh, I'm thinking it's just a harmless sedative in there—nothing dangerous. But I doubt that you need it."

For all Jane knew, that milk contained something prescribed by a doctor. But a hunch told her Dorothea really didn't need it.

When Jane returned from the bathroom, having poured the milk out and rinsed the glass and refilled it with water, Dorothea was eating. Jane took the glass to the bed and placed it on the tray. Then she sat next to the bed while Dorothea ate. It was odd to see the woman, almost like a child, pay attention to her food almost as though Jane were not in the room. But Jane knew that Dorothea was aware of her, so she began to talk.

"I think that what's been happening to Brandon all ties in to what happened in the other wing of the house. And also what happened to myself. You probably aren't aware of it, but somebody pushed me down the first night I was here, Dorothea. I went to Brandon's room and someone had switched off the night light. Or did I tell you already?"

If she were getting through to Dorothea, there certainly didn't appear to be any evidence of it. The woman just calmly ate her supper, not so much as glancing at Jane while she ate. It was as though Dorothea was in her private, personal little world, a world that nobody could enter unless she gave her permission.

Jane continued to chatter on. Somehow she felt that she must get through to the woman. She once again told her that she should never drink anything that was brought to her. Apparently, this had gotten through to Dorothea because several times she had found the glass of milk half hidden beneath the covers of her bed on the floor.

"I'll keep an eye on you and this room. When they bring your food, I'll make sure that you get some water to drink."

Jane stayed a short while with Dorothea, until the

woman had finished eating. Then she took the tray and placed it on the nightstand next to the bed.

She walked to the door. She glanced back before she left and she thought she saw a slight smile on Dorothea's face, but she couldn't be certain. It might just have been a trick of the lighting.

Too restless to go to her room, Jane walked down the corridor to the stairs. The house was quiet as usual and she felt a little nervous as she walked down the staircase. She glanced at the piano in the room near the stairs and couldn't help wondering how Hugh's wife might have looked sitting there and playing some song.

Jane walked past the piano room and toward the library. She always felt at ease around books. She had spent many happy hours when she was growing up in the public library back in Colorado, devouring every volume that she could find. But she was surprised when she walked into the paneled room to find Helene Kannon sitting there.

"Good evening, Miss Stewart," Helene said as she reached for the glass of iced tea she had placed on the coffee table before her. "You do get around, don't you?"

Jane could tell from the tone of Helene's voice that she was trying to rile her. She just smiled at the beauteous woman as she walked past her to the books.

"I thought I would find something new to read. And to check on the books that Brandon might enjoy at some later time."

"Oh, yes, your little angel. And how is the little imp getting along these days? Or have you had time to find out?"

Jane pivoted to look at Helene. "I don't understand what you are saying."

"Don't you? Well, I can speak plainer than that. You seem to be spending as much time with Brandon's father as you do with Brandon."

"Hugh has been very kind to me."

Helene's eyes narrowed menacingly. "Oh, I'm sure that he has. Do you use Brandon to get Hugh interested?"

Jane was getting annoyed with Helene. "Hugh is interested in his son's well-being."

Helene smirked. "Don't tell me that. Hugh hasn't cared for his son since the accident. That should be apparent even to someone like you, Miss Stewart."

"I don't think this conversation is getting us anywhere," Jane said. "If Hugh Hammett wants to take me and Brandon on a picnic or to a park, that is no concern of yours."

Helene got angrily to her feet. "Oh, isn't it? I've warned you before, Miss Stewart, to stay away from Hugh. He's mine and I mean to marry him. And I won't let anything interfere with that. I usually get what I set my mind on."

"And you've set your mind on Hugh Hammett."

"That's right."

"I doubt that Hugh feels the same way about you. Or does that matter to you?" Jane said.

Helene clenched her fists and pivoted and stalked out of the library. Jane knew that Helene was capable of anything. Then she thought of the initials she had seen on the lid of the box that Rhea had held in her hands before she put something or other into Dorothea's glass.

Maybe Helene was trying to do away with Dorothea so that Hugh would be free to marry her. It made sense, an awful, terrible sense. And Jane somehow could not quite believe it. Not quite. Jane turned her attention back to the wall of books. Perhaps she could forget all about Helene Kannon and her spiteful ways by reading a good book.

Jane selected one and sat down on the sofa. Just as she opened the book, she felt the presence of someone in the doorway. She glanced up from the volume and saw Mrs. March standing there.

"Yes, Mrs. March?" Jane said because it was apparent that the woman wasn't going to speak. "Is there anything the matter?"

Mrs. March continued to stare at her for a moment and then she said, "How long are you going to be here in this house, Miss Stewart?"

It was such an unexpected remark that Jane just gaped at the woman for a second or two. Then she said, "As long as I'm needed. And that depends on Brandon."

"You shouldn't stay," Mrs. March said. "Brandon can't be helped. You're just wasting your time."

"I don't agree with you," Jane said, feeling somewhat uneasy in the woman's presence. "As a matter of fact, Brandon has improved considerably since I first met him."

"Very well," Mrs. March said. "But don't say I didn't warn you."

With these words, the housekeeper turned and went away. Jane sat there looking at the doorway. She wondered why the housekeeper wanted her out of the way so much. She certainly was no threat to the woman's position.

Jane wondered what had prompted Mrs. March to be so forward with her. She had actually warned Jane to leave. With a sigh, Jane added the woman to her list of suspects.

Jane decided that she wouldn't stay in the library any longer. She would go upstairs and check on Brandon and then go to her room. At least she felt safe in her own room. As she left the library, she was in such deep thought that the book slipped from her grasp and fell to the carpeted floor.

Stooping down to pick it up, she heard the voice of Edgar Carrol coming from a room not far from where she knelt. He was obviously talking to someone on the telephone. Jane could only make out bits and pieces of the conversation.

"Don't worry. . . . I'll have the money for you . . . won't be long now. . . . Just give me a little more time . . ."

Jane didn't wait to hear any more. She grabbed the book and hurried upstairs. She wished that she hadn't heard the conversation. Obviously Edgar Carrol was in some kind of trouble. And that trouble was connected in some way with money.

Jane's mind was beginning to whirl with all the impressions that she had been picking up since coming to The Towers.

She went directly to Brandon's room and saw that he was sleeping soundly. Then she hurried to her own room in a fearful state of mind.

Chapter Seventeen

Now that she was in her room, Jane felt a certain comfort and security. There were such strange people living here, and each one seemed to have a motive for harming Dorothea.

Jane couldn't help but dwell on the conversation she had just overheard between Edgar Carrol and somebody. She didn't want her imagination to run away with itself, yet he had sounded so threatening and mysterious on the telephone. She already had gone over in her mind what Edgar Carrol's motives might be, and hearing the conversation just added to them.

Jane was about to get ready for bed when there was a rapping on her door. It was not just a gentle, slow tempo, but had an urgency to it. For a moment Jane just stood there trying to decide whether or not she would answer the rapping. Then it sounded again and she took a deep breath and walked over to the door.

She was startled to find Edgar Carrol standing there.

They stared at each other for a moment, Jane feeling a lump form in her throat.

Then Mr. Carrol spoke. "Please excuse me if I

caught you at a bad time, Miss Stewart."

Jane just stood there, not saying anything. She didn't trust her own voice.

"There is something that I wanted to talk over with you. It won't take but a moment. And we can talk right here. If you have the time."

Jane managed to nod her head. "What is it, Mr. Carrol?"

"It's about what you just heard when you were downstairs a short while ago. No, I'm not accusing you of eavesdropping. I understand that you just happened to be passing. You see, I was talking to a business associate of mine. He loaned a woman some money not too long ago, a great deal of money, and she has been procrastinating in paying him back. Since I know the woman better than he, I took it upon myself to remind her of the money that she owed. I was afraid that when you heard just part of the conversation, you might not understand the entire situation."

A feeling of relief spread through Jane's body and she felt somewhat embarrassed that she had been harboring such bad thoughts about Edgar Carrol.

"I really didn't mean to listen. It just happened that I dropped my book outside the room where you were making your call."

Mr. Carrol smiled. This was the first time she had ever seen the man smile and it changed his entire appearance. There was nothing threatening or frightening about this Mr. Carrol.

"You know, I've been watching you, Miss Stewart, and I think you are a person that one can trust. You appear to be a sincere and honest girl. A long time ago, Dorothea's husband and I were close friends. Then he married Dorothea and I have to confess that I found the marriage unsuitable. That was before I got to know and understand Dorothea. Anyway, in recent months she invited me for a while. I came to The Towers to watch over her. But as you can see, I didn't do too good a job of that. That's why I haven't left this place. When I know that Dorothea is completely safe, then I will go about my business."

It was such a surprising confession and so direct that Jane believed every word that Edgar Carrol was saying.

"I believe you," she said. "And I understand why you are here."

"You take care of yourself," Edgar said as he glanced around. "I wouldn't want anything to happen to you. Well, I'd best be going now. Thank you for hearing me out."

Edgar Carrol walked to his room then, and Jane closed her door behind him. At least that was one person she could cross off her list of suspects. She had certainly figured Edgar Carrol wrong.

Jane wondered if she had been mistaken about her suspicions of the other occupants of the house.

As Jane shed her clothing and put on a pair of pajamas, she thought about Edgar Carrol and what he had said to her. She was thankful that he no longer held a grudge against Dorothea. And it was touching to Jane that he cared so much for the old woman that he would spend so much time at the house.

Picking up the book she had taken from the library, she curled up in bed and tried to focus her attention on the words. At first she was successful and got caught up in the flow of the narrative. Then she found that she was beginning to reread a sentence here and there and finally that she was just staring at the open book and not really reading anything.

Casting the book aside, Jane lay back on the pillows and stared at the ceiling. She just wasn't sleepy. Her mind was a jumble of thoughts and images. She tried to sort out the pieces of the puzzle that danced around in her brain in a fragmented way.

First there was little Brandon. From all that she had been told by the people living here, except for Reba and Raymond, Brandon was fully capable of pushing that wheelchair down the stairs. Yet she hadn't been able to find that awful part of his nature that was so apparent to everyone else. To Jane, Brandon appeared to be a frightened, withdrawn little boy to whom something terrible had happened.

There had been the episode in his bedroom the first night that Jane had come to The Towers. She had not been mistaken. Someone had waited for her to come in and turn on Brandon's night light. Then that person had pushed her down, probably hoping that she would strike her head and be frightened into leaving the house.

Then there had been the boulder that had come crashing down, just missing her. And there was the time she went into the east wing and was locked out of the house. All of these things added up to one thing: someone was trying to drive Jane away from The Towers.

Yet she knew that she would not leave. She just couldn't run out on Brandon—or Dorothea, for that matter. They both needed her. Somehow they were linked together. They knew something, something terrible and awful. Something that kept both of them silent about what had happened that day to Dorothea when she and Brandon were in the east wing. Who, if not Brandon, had been the one responsible for the accident?

The very first person who came to Jane's mind was Helene Kannon. Jane had seen Rhea open the box and take something out and put it in Dorothea's milk. And Jane had seen the initials in the mirror. Very plainly they had been H.K.

And hadn't Reba told her that Rhea's bank account was growing? Perhaps Helene had paid Rhea to put something in Dorothea's milk, something that would keep her in a confused state of mind. That certainly made sense.

Still, Jane thought, she could hardly overlook the other people in the house. There was David Hammett, for example. He certainly had made it perfectly clear that he was only waiting until Dorothea's death so that he would gain financially. Lorene, Jane felt, probably just went along with her husband. However, Jane knew that she couldn't totally dismiss Lorene. Even though she might appear to be a delicate woman, there was a certain steely strength about her that had to be reckoned with.

Jane tried not to include Hugh Hammett in all this, but there was no way that she could overlook him. He certainly did not care for his young son as he should—even though Jane felt that in his heart he truly loved his only child. But could it have been Hugh who had been in the east wing that day and done such a terrible thing to his own mother? Jane shuddered at such thoughts.

Turning on her side, she stared across the room at the far wall, but she saw nothing.

Her thoughts now were of Katherine Hammett, Hugh's tall, cold older sister. She was still an enigma to Jane. Even now when she thought about Katherine, she couldn't quite make out the woman's features. As she began to dwell on Katherine, there was a quick rap again on the door.

Getting to her feet, Jane walked to the door wondering if Edgar Carrol might have come back for another quick talk session. But she was surprised to see Reba standing in the dimly lighted corridor.

"I know it's late, but I thought maybe you might like to talk for a while," Reba said.

There was a pleading look in the girl's face that made Jane smile at her and say, "Not that late. Come on in, Reba."

Quickly, as though she felt that she were being watched, Reba entered the bedroom. "I guess I could have brought some coffee or something. Maybe I'm getting out of my place by coming here, but I just felt kind of creepy tonight. You know the feeling. Like something is about to happen. The way you feel just before a big storm."

"I know what you mean," Jane said as she sat on the bed and Reba sat on a chair not far from her.

"Sometimes this old place gets on my nerves," Reba went on. "And tonight is one of those times."

"Why tonight, I wonder?"

"It was like this the day the accident happened," Reba said. "Kind of like you could feel something in the air."

Jane could see that Reba was getting herself into a state of nerves. She was uneasy herself, but she didn't want to let that feeling show.

"I should tell you something," Jane said. "Because I think I can trust you."

Reba leaned forward eagerly in her chair. She had such an open honesty about her that it was difficult to believe that she was the twin sister of Rhea.

"Please tell me."

"When I went to Brandon's room tonight, I found that one of his ships had been smashed. Someone was in the room before I got there and just demolished the model."

Reba's eyes grew wide with interest and shock. "How terrible. Little Brandon just loves those models. Who could have done such a terrible thing?"

"I think it was the same person who pushed Dorothea down the stairs."

Reba gasped. It was the first time that Jane had

ever hinted that the accident might have been caused by someone other than Brandon.

"Who do you think it is?"

Jane shook her head. "I don't know. I have a lot of different ideas, but I have no proof. After getting to know Brandon, I simply can't make myself believe that he's capable of harming anyone."

Reba nodded. Jane could tell by the look in the young girl's eyes that she believed what Jane was saying. "That's what I felt all along. Only, I didn't think it was my place to say anything."

"You weren't by any chance on this floor earlier this evening?"

"No. I was busy downstairs practically all night, until I decided to come up here and see you. Why?"

"If you had been, then maybe you might have seen someone going in or coming out of Brandon's room."

Reba sighed. "I wish I could help you, Jane, but I'm afraid I can't."

"That's all right. Whoever has been doing these things is bound to slip up."

They chatted for a little longer, and then Reba excused herself.

After Reba had gone, Jane reached for her book once more and tried to focus her attention on what was printed on its pages. But Reba's words kept coming back to her and interfering with her concentration.

Yes, there was something intangible in the atmosphere of the house tonight. A sense of danger, of something about to happen.

Jane stared at the page of the book she was reading and the words made no sense to her whatsoever. She placed the book on the nightstand and switched off the light. The room immediately was pitched into darkness and that darkness seemed to take on a living quality. Jane slipped beneath the covers on the bed and pulled them up to her chin.

She closed her eyes and tried to fall asleep. It was an impossible thing for her to do. She tossed and turned and tried everything she could think of to court sleep. It was no good.

Reaching out, Jane turned on the lamp and sat up. She glanced at her watch and saw that it was quite late. And the night seemed to stretch endlessly ahead of her.

"I have to do something to get some sleep," Jane said aloud. "Maybe a glass of warm milk will do it. That always helped in the past."

Tossing the covers aside, she reached for her robe which was at the foot of her bed and slipped her arms through the sleeves. She padded across the carpet and opened the door to the hallway. Glancing out, she saw that nobody was there, and it was more dimly lighted than usual. Or so it seemed.

Jane gathered her robe around her for some sort of protection as she headed toward the staircase. She glanced over her shoulder to see if anyone might be lurking in the shadows. As far as she could tell, there was nobody there. Still, when she neared the stairs, she felt the presence of eyes watching her. It was a creepy feeling and Jane hurried down rapidly.

When she reached the landing, she thought she heard a noise coming from the hallway that branched off the main corridor. Slowly she moved in the direction of the noise, wondering if she were doing the right thing. She didn't feel in the least bit brave, but she was curious as to who might be downstairs at this hour of the night.

There was nobody in the hallway and she hurried to the kitchen. She poured some milk into a pan and waited until it began to warm up on the stove. As she stood there, she glanced across the counter and her attention was focused on a small box. It was the same box she had seen Rhea use before she went into Dorothea's room. As Jane moved toward the box, the lights went out and she was plunged into darkness.

Chapter Eighteen

"Who's there?" Jane called because she felt the presence of someone else in the kitchen. There was a sound, a movement close to her, and then whoever was with her was gone.

Jane tried to remember where the light switch was, but she was completely disoriented in the darkness. She groped frantically around and her hand touched the refrigerator door. Easing her hand down the door, she touched the handle on the refrigerator and flung it open.

By the light cast from the open refrigerator, she was able to find the switch on the wall. When she flicked the switch, she quickly looked around the kitchen, but now no one else was there.

Her scrutiny of the kitchen finally turned to the counter top where the little box with the initials H.K. had rested. She was not really surprised to find that the box was gone. Then she pivoted quickly and hurried out of the kitchen, slamming the refrigerator door as she left.

Then Jane heard the sound of someone at the top of the stairs. In his or her haste to get away, the person who had taken the box must have bumped against one of the oil paintings on the walls next to the stairs.

Jane immediately rushed to the staircase and, as she ascended, she heard the sound of a door closing on the second floor. By the time she reached the landing, there was nobody in the hallway. It could have been anyone who had followed her down to the kitchen and taken the box.

Not anyone, Jane corrected herself, but Helene Kannon. She must have been the person who had followed her and waited for her chance to recover the box. Rhea must have accidentally left the box in the kitchen and Helene had gone there to make certain that Jane didn't find it.

Reba had told Jane where everyone slept in the house, so she knew which room belonged to Helene Kannon. Jane went directly to the room and rapped on the door. When Helene came to the door, which would be quite quickly, Jane would know that she had been the one who had taken the box. She would see it on her face.

Jane waited impatiently and then her knuckles tapped on the surface of the door once again. The door finally opened and Helene Kannon stood there. It was obvious from her appearance that she had just gotten out of bed. She was barely awake.

When she saw Jane, she said, "What do you want?"

It was an awkward situation. Jane quickly thought of a reason for awakening Helene, since it was obvious that Helene hadn't been the person who had switched off the light and taken the box in the kitchen.

"I'm sorry. I didn't think you would be asleep yet. But I have a slight headache and I seem to have run out of aspirin."

This was not an untrue statement, since Jane felt a throbbing in her head that had started when Reba had been in her room earlier.

Helene made a sigh of impatience but disappeared somewhere in her room and returned with two small pills. "Is there anything else?"

"No, this is fine. Sorry I interrupted your sleep."

Without another word, Helene quickly shut the door in Jane's face, and Jane stood there with the aspirin in her hand. She must have been mistaken when she thought that it was Helene who had come into the kitchen. But if it wasn't Helene, then why had someone taken that box that so obviously belonged to Helene? Then from somewhere in the back of her mind, Jane began to wonder about the box. There was something wrong with what she was thinking, something not quite right. At the moment she could not determine what it was.

If it hadn't been Helene who had taken the box, then it must have been Rhea. She undoubtedly had left it on the counter top and then had to return for it. Jane made a quick decision to go to her room and confront the woman. Even though it was growing later and later, she felt that she should strike while the iron was hot.

Reba had told her that she and her sister had two rooms off the kitchen where they slept. Jane walked away from Helene's door and once again headed down the stairs to the lower floor. The eerie feeling that Reba had spoken of earlier that evening was still in the air. Jane knew that unseen eyes were watching her every movement, and at this point she really didn't care. She felt compelled to find out who was at the bottom of the mystery surrounding The Towers.

When she arrived at the foot of the stairs, she turned and walked toward the two rooms that Reba had told her about. Jane was not certain which room belonged to Reba and which room was Rhea's. So she just took a deep breath when she came to the first door and knocked quickly.

She stood there for what seemed hours until she saw the knob on the door begin to turn. Slowly the door opened and in the dim light stood Rhea. She blinked at the light cast by the hall lighting and focused her eyes.

"Miss Stewart! What are you doing here?" she said in a flat, unemotional tone of voice.

"There is something I must talk over with you, Rhea," Jane said with as much authority as she could muster.

"At this hour? Let it wait until morning."

She started to close the door, but Jane held out her hand to prevent it.

"It won't take long. There are some questions I want answers to."

Rhea took her hand off the doorknob and crossed her arms. She looked defiantly at Jane. "You're no better than the rest of the help. What right have you to come around waking me up out of a sound sleep?"

"Were you sleeping?"

"Of course, I was. I don't spend the night prowling around this place like some people I know."

Jane wasn't about to be put off by the girl's surly behavior. She felt that Rhea was just trying to put her on the defensive.

"You weren't by any chance in the kitchen just a little while ago, were you?"

Jane studied Rhea's face for any reaction. There was none except for a slight tightening of her thin lips.

"No, I wasn't in the kitchen a little while ago. Is that why you came down here to see me?"

"That and for other reasons," Jane said, wondering if again she might have been mistaken in her thinking. "I was in the kitchen not too long ago and there was a small box on the counter top. Just as I started to go over to the box, somebody turned out the light and took the box."

There was a slight look of alarm in Rhea's eyes, so Jane knew that she had struck home.

"What has that got to do with me?" Rhea said in a voice that had lost some of its edge.

"I thought perhaps that you would know something about it."

"Well, I don't. You must be seeing things."

"I don't think so. You know about the box, don't you, Rhea? As a matter of fact, I saw you with that very same box outside Dorothea's room."

Rhea's hands had joined together and she was squeezing them so tightly that the knuckles were white. Jane knew that she could only go so far in her accusations, so she waited for Rhea to answer.

Finally, Reba's sister spoke. It was in a low, deadly voice. "If you know what's good for you, Miss Stewart, you will forget all about that box. That's all I'm going to say to you."

Without another word, Rhea slammed the door in Jane's face. That was the second time tonight that that had happened to her. She was tempted to bang again on the door, but she knew that she would get nothing further from Rhea at this time.

At least she had gotten the surly girl to admit that she knew something about the box. And Jane felt certain that Helene Kannon was involved in all this too. Only, she couldn't understand why Helene had been in her room when the box was taken from the kitchen. If it had been Rhea, there was no way that Jane would be able to find that out tonight.

She turned and walked away from Rhea's room, feeling a mixture of satisfaction and puzzlement. If Helene hadn't taken the box—or Rhea—then who had it been?

As Jane walked back toward the kitchen, she suddenly remembered the milk that she had put on to heat. With a sigh of relief, she found that she had had enough presence of mind to remove the milk from the stove after she had switched on the light. She got a glass from the cupboard and poured the milk from the pan into it. It was still warm as she walked over to the table and sat down.

Just as she was about to take a sip, she felt the presence of someone else in the room and, glancing toward the door, she saw Hugh Hammett standing there.

"You're up rather late, aren't you, Jane?" he said in a curious tone of voice.

"I couldn't sleep," Jane quickly replied. "I thought a glass of milk might help me."

"It is a rather restless night," Hugh said as he came over to the table. He was still dressed in the clothing that he had worn at dinnertime.

Apparently, Hugh felt the uneasiness of the house tonight too and hadn't gone to bed yet.

"Reba seemed to think so too," said Jane after taking a sip from the glass. "She and I had a long talk this evening. She seemed to feel that there was something strange about the house tonight."

Hugh arched an eyebrow. "As a matter of fact, it was on a night very much like this that the accident happened. Only, it was much earlier in the evening. Brandon was still up. He kept insisting on taking Mother for a ride, as he called it. If only he hadn't done that. But we can't live in the past, can we?"

Jane didn't say what was on her mind, that everyone in this house did seem to live in the past. The accident was as fresh in their minds as though it had just happened the night before.

"We shouldn't," Jane said. "Did anyone go with Brandon and your mother to the east wing?"

Hugh glared at her. "Of course not. They were alone."

"Are you sure?"

Hugh's eyes seemed to be boring right through her skull. Jane was feeling uncertain about being alone with him. Yet she had to get to the bottom of this once and for all. So she plunged on.

"Somebody might have followed them to the east wing. Somebody might have waited until Brandon wasn't looking or was away from the chair and then pushed your mother down the stairs."

"That's monstrous," Hugh said, his eyes narrowing into thin slits.

"It's also monstrous to think that your son could do such a thing to his grandmother. Brandon loves Dorothea. He wouldn't do anything to harm her."

"You don't know my son. You were not there when it happened."

"That's true. I wasn't. Were you?"

Hugh Hammett got to his feet. "I think this conversation has gone as far as it should. We'll discuss this in the morning."

Jane knew she was on dangerous ground, but she couldn't stop now. She was too close to some truth, to something that might help.

"What's wrong with talking now? Hugh, Brandon did not push your mother down the stairs. He just couldn't have done such a terrible thing."

"You seem very sure of yourself. If Brandon didn't, then who did?"

Jane sighed. She wished that she had an answer to that question, but all she had were just suspicions. "I don't know. But I just feel that it wasn't Brandon."

There was an ironic twist to Hugh's mouth. "You shouldn't go on just feelings, Jane. Feelings aren't to be trusted."

With that, Hugh left her alone. She turned her attention back to the glass of milk, but she found that she had a difficult time swallowing it. Why was it that every time she was around Hugh Hammett, she got this peculiar feeling in the pit of her stomach? Why did her knees feel shaky whenever he was near her?

She fought the idea that she might be in love with him. After all, she was just here to help Brandon. She meant nothing to Hugh Hammett. Or did she? Sometimes he could be so compassionate and charming. Yet on the other hand, he could be changeable and like somebody she hardly knew.

All she really knew for certain was that she had been here in this kitchen when somebody had come in, turned off the light, and made off with that peculiar box. Even though Helene Kannon's initials were on it, Jane felt almost positive that she had truly awakened the sleeping woman. So it couldn't have been Helene who had been in here.

Therefore, it must have been Rhea. After all, Jane had seen her in the mirror with the box in her hand just before she had gone into Dorothea's room. But if it was Rhea, then whom had she heard at the top of the stairs?

Jane took her glass to the sink and rinsed it. Then she switched off the light as she walked out of the kitchen. She wearily climbed the stairs to the second floor and started down the hallway. When she came to Dorothea's room, she decided to take a look in to make certain she was sleeping. But when she looked into the room, Dorothea was wide awake and she beckoned to Jane.

"Come in, Miss Stewart," the old woman said. "And shut that door behind you. We must talk."

Chapter Nineteen

Jane quickly closed the door behind her and looked at Dorothea. Her eyes were alert and there was a vitality about her that hadn't been there before. And she had spoken.

"Come closer," Dorothea said as she raised one hand and beckoned to Jane. "Sit here on the bed, beside me."

Obediently Jane moved toward the bed. This was such a surprise to her that she found herself almost staring with an open mouth at Hugh Hammett's mother. "You can speak. I thought you could all along."

"There is nothing wrong with my voice," Dorothea said, and there was a slight smile on her lips. "Although I'm sure that somebody in this house wishes that there were."

By this time, Jane had come to the bed and she sat down, still staring with bewilderment at the woman. She wondered why Dorothea had suddenly, after all this time, decided to speak up. She was very anxious to listen to all that the old woman had to say.

"I've been watching and studying you, Miss Stewart. May I call you Jane?"

"Please do."

"Very well then, Jane. As I said, I've been listening to what you've had to say and I've been judging your actions. I had to be sure of you before I spoke to you."

"And are you sure of me?"

The smile deepened on Dorothea's face. "Very sure. You really do care about my grandson and his well-being. That wasn't the case with the others. They were such skitty, silly girls. All they seemed to care about was their salary and living in this house."

Jane didn't know how to respond to this, so she just kept silent.

"Oh, I was aware of them. Even though sometimes I wasn't thinking too clearly. That was probably because Rhea was doping my milk. If it hadn't been for you, I might have gone on taking that glass of milk more often and never knowing that it was harming me. Though I did have my own suspicions. That girl, Rhea, I never did trust her. Not a bit like her sister. But she'll be taken care of before long."

Jane again just listened to the woman. Even though Dorothea had not totally recovered from her accident and was still in a weakened condition, there was a spark of vitality about her that hadn't been there before.

"You know when I had my accident, the police came, but they couldn't get anything out of Brandon. Finally, Hugh persuaded them that it had been an accident and that he would keep an eye on Brandon."

For the first time Jane spoke. "Do you think we

should call the police now? After all, someone has been tampering with the milk."

"Would it do any good now? I haven't touched any liquids that have been brought me in days. It would just be our word against whoever is doing all this."

"I suppose you are right. But if anything like that happens again, I am going to call the authorities."

Dorothea looked fondly at Jane. "You have been good for this house, Jane. That's why I feel I can trust you."

"Do you feel at all like talking any more? I don't want you to overdo."

"Nonsense," Dorothea said in a huff. "I feel just fine. And I think it's time that I spoke up."

Jane sat quietly. She knew that what Dorothea had to say was very important and might possibly shed some light on the mystery of The Towers. The eeriness of the night was still in the air, and Jane felt a slight chill that had nothing to do with the temperature outside.

"The day Brandon took me to the east wing, or rather the evening, was very much like tonight. I don't suppose that you've noticed the strange atmosphere here at the house tonight."

"Not only myself but Reba as well. She mentioned something about the house giving her the creeps tonight."

There was a faint chuckle from Dorothea. "Reba is so unlike her sister. She's such a direct and honest person. Yes, I can believe that she said that. And it's true. There was the same sort of something in the air that night.

"Brandon had come to my room and wanted to take me for a ride. I've always found it difficult to deny him anything. That was when he was such an apple of his father's eye. How things have changed since that last night." Dorothea paused for a moment, as though she were reflecting on something in the far distant past.

"After he begged me to let him take me out of my room, I finally agreed. As we went through the hallway, I had the feeling that we were not alone, that someone was following us. It made me uneasy and a little frightened. When we got to the east wing, Brandon left me near the stairs. I remember that he was playing with a ball that he had found in his pocket. So it couldn't have been Brandon who pushed the chair down the stairs. It couldn't have been him."

Jane leaned forward and took one of Dorothea's hands in her own. "Why didn't you tell the police this?"

"Really, I couldn't, dear. I was unconscious for the longest time and in a state of shock for days. I couldn't have spoken. And then I was afraid to speak up. I began to hear what was happening to Brandon, how he was changing, how frightened he had become. Then I knew that whoever had done this thing to me had gotten to Brandon and had threatened him. If I said anything about what happened in the east wing, I was afraid that something awful would happen to my grandson. And I just couldn't live with that."

Jane could understand now why Dorothea hadn't spoken up before. It was fear, fear of what might happen to Brandon.

"You did the right thing in not speaking up," Jane said in a soothing tone of voice. "You might have spoken to the wrong person and that person could have harmed Brandon."

"Then you believe that it was someone besides Brandon who pushed me down the stairs too," Dorothea said, and there was a relieved note in her voice.

"Yes, I do. After meeting Brandon and being with him, I just couldn't imagine that he was capable of such a terrible thing. I knew it had to be someone else. Someone who waited for me the first night I arrived here and pushed me down, causing me to strike my head."

Dorothea asked, "You don't think Rhea put that stuff in my drink on her own, do you, Jane?"

Jane shook her head. "She was just acting under orders, I think. As a matter of fact, I saw the box of stuff that she used and it had Helene Kannon's initials on the top of it."

Dorothea slowly shook her head. "I just don't believe it. No, I don't doubt what you saw. It's just that I can't imagine Helene doing such a thing. What would be the purpose?"

"I think she's in love with Hugh," Jane said flatly.

"That's ridiculous. Helene Kannon isn't in love

with anyone but herself. And as far as Hugh is concerned, he certainly isn't fond of her. If she is behind all this, then we haven't found the motive for her actions."

To Jane, these words from Dorothea had a strange effect. It was as though a door had suddenly been flung wide open. Still, Jane couldn't help but wonder if perhaps Hugh was behind what had happened to Dorothea. She hesitated to say this to the woman since she didn't know what Dorothea's reaction might be to the idea of her son trying to harm her.

"I must tell you something, Dorothea. Tonight I went down to the kitchen for some milk. It always helps me sleep. I saw that same box on the counter. Just as I moved toward it, someone turned off the light. When I got it back on again, the box was gone. And I heard someone going up the stairs to this floor."

"Who do you think it was?"

"Naturally, I thought it was Helene. But when I went to her room and knocked on the door, it took her a long time to answer. And she really did look as though I had just awakened her."

Dorothea was quiet for a moment or two, deep in thought. "Then it wasn't Helene. It might have been Lorene or David."

"Do you really think so?"

"David is a scamp. Always has been. He's never held down a job in his entire life. I think a good, hardworking job would do wonders for him. As for Lorene, she's a sweet girl, but I've never gotten to know her very well. She could be capable of anything."

Jane had to agree with Dorothea, even though Lorene had been nicer to her than anyone else in the house, except for Reba. Yet it was David whom she felt was more capable of foul play than his wife. Again Jane didn't mention this. After all, David was her son too and blood was thicker than water.

"It's a mystery, that's for certain," Dorothea said as she lay back on the pillows.

Suddenly she looked very old and very tired. But as Jane leaned forward to look at her, the old woman seemed to gain some strength from somewhere and the tiredness quickly left her face.

"You must be very careful here, Jane," Dorothea said. "I think you are learning too much about all this and it could be dangerous for you."

Jane reached out and patted Dorothea on the hand. "Don't worry about me. I can take care of myself. But I won't take any foolish chances."

Dorothea smiled at Jane. "You are the daughter I really wanted. Oh, not that I don't love Katherine. But she has always been a stranger to me. She's so cool and aloof and so practical about everything. There's just no warmth to her. I guess maybe it was my fault. I should have been more demonstrative when she was growing up."

"Don't blame yourself," Jane said. "You did what you thought was best for your children, I'm sure."

Dorothea shook her head. "No, that really isn't true, Jane. I was never one to speak out and show any authority. Or warmth. So Katherine became what I should have been. It's almost as though we've reversed roles."

"Try not to think about that now," Jane said in a gentle tone of voice. "Why don't you get some rest. I'll be in my room in case you might want me. I'll leave your door and mine open just a bit so that I'll be able to hear you."

"I think you're right," Dorothea said. "I'm glad you're here at The Towers, Jane. Good night."

Jane sat on the bed until Dorothea closed her eyes, and then she got to her feet and walked cautiously out of the bedroom. She left the door open as she had promised and went to her room.

Not bothering to remove the robe she was wearing, Jane stretched out on the bed. She found that she was sleepy now that she had had her conversation with Dorothea Hammett. All of her suspicions had been confirmed tonight with that talk. She was relieved that someone besides herself believed in the innocence of Brandon.

Dorothea had said that he had been playing when the accident had happened. But should it be called an accident now? It was a deliberate act of someone to harm and possibly kill Dorothea.

Jane turned on her side and slowly her eyelids began to close. It had been a long and exhausting day. The strange atmosphere of the house had not thinned, but Jane was too tired now to really care. She closed her eyes and felt herself beginning to drift off to sleep.

She hadn't been asleep very long when she awoke suddenly—and with the knowledge that something was wrong. She sniffed the air and there was the faint odor of something burning. Jane heard voices in the distance and she sprang out of bed and ran to the door. Stepping out into the corridor, she saw that there was a thin layer of gray smoke that hung in the air.

"Where's that coming from?" came a voice that she recognized as David Hammett's.

"Down here!" another voice answered, and this came from Hugh Hammett.

Jane hurried through the hazy smoke that was a nuisance and not choking. She saw figures of other people ahead of her, and there was a babble of voices.

"Someone get some water," David called out, and Jane bumped into Lorene, who was rushing past her to get back to her room.

"Where is it coming from?" David demanded.

"This closet," was Hugh's answer, and Jane found herself standing next to Hugh, who had opened a closet facing the staircase. Smoke rose from the floor of the closet and Hugh took a jacket and covered the pile of rags from which the haze was rising. By the time Lorene came with a pitcher of water, the emergency was over.

"Just what caused this?" David asked as he looked over Hugh's shoulder.

"This pile of rags," Hugh said as he sifted through the remains of the fire with his foot. "It must have been spontaneous combustion."

Jane wondered if that was the truth, but she didn't feel like asking at this time. Everyone was too much upset about what had happened for her to add to it at the moment.

"Is it safe to go back to bed?" David asked in a nervous tone of voice.

"Of course, it is," Hugh replied. "Give me that pitcher of water, Lorene, and I'll just make doubly certain that it's out."

There was no telltale hissing sound as Hugh poured the contents of the pitcher over the rags, so Jane felt assured that the fire had been extinguished.

"I'd better check on Dorothea," Jane said. "Just in case she might be awake and wondering what happened."

"You do that," Helene Kannon said in a sarcastic way, but Jane ignored her as she hurried to Dorothea's room. Dorothea was sitting up in bed, and her eyes were wide with fear and curiosity.

"What's happening out there?"

"Nothing to worry about," Jane said. "It was just some rags that caught fire. But Hugh has taken care of it. Everything's all right."

"I wonder," Dorothea said in a thoughtful voice, and then she said, "Quick, Jane, go check on Brandon. I have a strange feeling that something might be wrong."

Without hesitating, Jane spun around and dashed to Brandon's room. The night lamp was still on, but the covers on the young boy's bed had been hastily tossed aside and he was gone.

Chapter Twenty

"Brandon! Brandon! It's all right. The fire is out!" Jane called out, thinking that he might be hiding in the room. But there was no answer. She quickly looked in the closet and under the bed, but Brandon was nowhere to be found.

Jane hurried to Dorothea's room. She quickly told her about Brandon's disappearance. "Where could he have gone?"

A worried look was on Dorothea's face and she said, "Try the east wing. He might be there. Something tells me that's where he's gone."

Without questioning Dorothea, Jane ran from the bedroom. There was nobody in the corridor, but she still felt eyes following her movements as she scurried along.

Ahead of her loomed the east wing, dark and shadowy and intimidating. She suddenly recalled what had happened to her the last time she had been in that part of the house and a quick shiver went down her spine. But she pushed those thoughts from her mind. It was Brandon she must think about now. He was in danger. If he was in the east wing, he could be harmed. This spurred her on with renewed vigor and determination. She had no idea what she might encounter in that part of the house, but she must hurry and get there.

Within minutes she was in the east wing and she paused for a moment, looking around. She found that she had come to the staircase, the very stairs where the accident to Dorothea had occurred. She almost felt that she was reliving another moment in time. Only, she had not been present at that time.

"Brandon? Brandon?" she called out and her voice seemed to echo in the empty wing of the house. "It's Jane. Are you there?"

She waited and listened, listened for any sound of movement that would tell her that Brandon had come here. Then she saw something, a movement not far from where she stood. From out of the shadows stepped Brandon.

"Brandon! There you are," Jane cried as she hurried over to him. "I was so worried about you. You weren't frightened because of the fire, were you? It's all right. Your father put it out and there was no damage."

Brandon shook his head. "That didn't scare me. But she did."

"She? What are you talking about?"

Brandon was staring past Jane, as though he didn't see her. And she found that he was trembling as she put her arms around him.

"She told me that I shouldn't say anything. That she would punish me."

"Who said that to you, Brandon? Nobody will hurt you. I'm here to protect you."

Brandon shook his head. "I can't tell you. She comes into my room all the time. And she was the one who broke my ship. She's bad."

Jane held Brandon's shaking body close to her own. There was anger in her. Anger against whoever this woman was who was doing such terrible things to Brandon. She evidently had threatened him so badly that he was terrified to reveal her name. Jane had ideas of her own about whom it might be, but she had to calm Brandon down first. She had to reassure him that he was safe, that nobody would harm him.

Slowly as Jane held him, Brandon began to cease his trembling. Jane spoke soothing words to him to try and offer him as much comfort as she could. When she felt that he had calmed down, she released her hold on him and held him by the shoulders.

"Why did you come here, of all places, Brandon?"

The little boy looked into her eyes and stared at her for a moment or two, then said, "When the fire started, and I smelled smoke, I thought that she had done it. So I ran down here to get away from my room. I thought that she would come to my room while everyone was in the hallway."

Jane knew that she had to approach Brandon tactfully if she ever expected him to tell her who this woman was who was threatening him so.

"Then it wasn't your father who pushed your grandmother down those stairs," Jane said as she indicated the steps with a nod of her head.

Brandon shook his head. "No, but he thinks that

it was me. Only, I couldn't tell him who it really was."

Jane felt a surge of relief that it hadn't been Hugh who had done this terrible thing to Dorothea. In her heart she had always felt that he was incapable of such an act. Hugh was becoming more and more important in her life.

Only, she had no idea how he truly felt about her. He, at those times when he became compassionate and kind, might just have been that way because he felt sorry for her. Or he might have expressed himself that way out of gratitude to her because she was taking care of his son.

"So your Uncle David wasn't here that day either, am I right?"

Again Brandon shook his head. "Uncle David wasn't here either. Only, I think he believes I pushed Grandma down the stairs."

That took care of David Hammett, Jane thought and any other male who lived here at The Towers. That only left the women and Jane had to find out which one it was, for both Brandon's and her own sake.

"Brandon, will you tell me if it was Rhea who comes into your room? Is she the one who broke your ship and turns out the light in your room?"

At the mention of Rhea's name, Jane noticed that Brandon visibly flinched. But he slowly shook his head. "Rhea isn't the one. She's bad too. Not like Reba. Reba has always been nice to me. She plays with me the way you do. She's fun."

Jane smiled faintly at Brandon. She could tell that he thought a lot of the friendly, pleasant maid. She still had to pursue this while Brandon was in these surroundings. It might make him unknowingly reveal who the person was that pushed his grandmother down the stairs. At least she would try.

"What about Miss Kannon?" Jane asked. "Has she ever done anything bad to you? Was she here that day when the accident happened?"

Brandon quickly shook his head. "It wasn't her. She's too busy trying to get attention from my daddy to notice me."

Jane realized then that Helene's activities as far as Hugh Hammett were concerned hadn't gone unnoticed by his young son. And she remembered what Dorothea had said about Helene. Neither one of them seemed to care too much for the beautiful woman.

"I guess we'd better be going back to the other wing," Jane finally said. "You'll be safe there. The fire is out and nobody will harm you."

"Are you certain of that, Miss Stewart," came a soft but firm voice from behind her. Jane was looking at Brandon and she saw that he was staring with terrified eyes at whoever had spoken.

Jane knew that voice, a woman's voice. She had heard it often enough since she had been at the house.

Jane slowly rose from her crouching position and turned to see Katherine Hammett standing in the dim light of the corridor.

"So it was you." Jane spoke in as level a voice as she could muster.

A slight laugh, with an hysterical edge to it, came from Katherine's lips. She was holding one hand behind her back, and the other hand was tightly clenched. She took a step forward and the light—what little there was of it—fell upon her face. Katherine's eyes had a wild, frantic look to them. Otherwise her features were the same, stoic and stone-hard.

"Yes, it was me. You really shouldn't have come here, Miss Stewart. There is nothing that you can do for Brandon. But you did come, and you did interfere. I suspected you'd be the type to do that from the minute you arrived here."

Jane placed herself between Katherine and Brandon. She would not allow this woman to do any further harm to the little boy. At the moment she was thinking of how she and Brandon would get away from Katherine. Jane was not frightened of the woman, since she felt that she was strong enough to fight her off, if it came to that.

"You were the one who was in Brandon's room the first night I came here," Jane said.

"Of course. I thought you would be as easily frightened as the others. It didn't take much to send those other girls packing. But I didn't reckon on you being so stubborn."

Jane kept her eyes on Katherine for any sudden movement. If she did decide to rush her and Brandon, she would be ready to bolt and run with the little boy.

"And I suppose you followed us that day when

we went on the picnic and pushed that boulder down from the top of the cliff. I didn't think Brandon had the strength to do that."

"That's right. Just another one of my hints to get you to leave The Towers. I didn't plan on you being so quick on your feet. And I locked you out of that room in this wing. I followed you that day and saw an opportunity to try and frighten you once more. It's too bad that David came along when he did and heard you out there. I'm sure that if he hadn't, you wouldn't have decided to remain here any longer."

Jane kept her eyes on Katherine. She could see from her eyes that the woman was unbalanced, that she was dangerous, capable of anything.

"I thought it was Helene Kannon," said Jane as her thoughts began to clear and the pieces of the puzzle fell into place. "When I looked in the mirror and saw Rhea with that box of stuff, I mistook the initials on the box. They weren't H.K. but actually your initials Katherine Hammett. Naturally, I would have been confused."

"Yes, Rhea has been very well paid for her services. And I thought you were becoming suspicious. That's why I followed you tonight when you went to the kitchen. Rhea had left the box on the counter and I had to get it before you found out who the box really belonged to."

"So Rhea is in on this too," Jane said with a trace of scorn in her voice.

"Rhea is greedy. She will do anything for money.

Not a bit like her sister. Rhea has been very useful to me."

Jane felt that she had to keep Katherine talking as long as possible so that she and Brandon might have a chance to escape.

"So you started that fire tonight as a diversion in order to try and get to Brandon again."

"That's right. He is getting too attached to you and I was afraid that he might confide in you."

"But why did you do all these things? Why did you push Dorothea down the stairs?"

Katherine laughed again; it had a terrifying edge to it. "I wanted her out of the way. I've wanted her money for years. I was tired of being shut up here in this place. I'm not getting any younger and I wanted my money so that I could get away. But you almost ruined that. But not quite."

With these words Katherine brought her hand out from behind her back; she was holding a poker in it and she raised it above her head. Jane dashed forward and grabbed Katherine's arm.

"Run, Brandon, quick. Get away," she screamed and the little boy dashed down the corridor.

Jane struggled with Katherine, but the woman seemed to have superhuman strength and finally she flung Jane against the wall near the stairs. Katherine had cut off any avenue of escape as she started toward Jane with the poker upraised in her hand. Jane braced herself for the blow that was to come.

Then she heard a voice from behind Katherine

shout, "Drop that, Katherine. Put that poker down."

It was Hugh. Katherine, caught off guard by the voice, turned, but in doing so she lost her balance and there was a hideous scream as she toppled down the stairs.

Before Jane knew it, Hugh had taken her into his arms. "Oh, my darling, are you all right? I was on my way here when I met Brandon. He told me what was happening."

Jane nestled her head against Hugh's chest and felt his strong, muscular arms cradling her. The nightmare was over and she suddenly felt tears welling in her eyes.

"I'm fine, just fine," Jane said. "And Brandon is safe."

"Yes, he is, thanks to you," Hugh said as he tilted her head back with his hand and gently brushed her lips with his own. "I've been such a fool. Blaming Brandon for what Katherine did. I only hope it isn't too late to make it up to him."

"I'm sure it isn't," Jane managed to say as she gazed into Hugh's tender eyes.

"I might need help. Someone to be with me and him. Someone on a permanent basis."

Jane stared at Hugh and saw that a slight smile had touched his lips. "But I don't think I could work here that long."

"But if you were Mrs. Hugh Hammett, that would be a different story, wouldn't it?"

"Oh, Hugh, are you asking me to marry you?"

"If you'll have me. I think I've loved you since

the minute I saw you in Brandon's room."

"Of course I will. But what of Katherine?"

Together they went down the stairs. Katherine had struck her head, but she was alive. Hugh carried her to her room and there they discussed what had to be done with her. Hugh explained that Katherine had shown signs of being unbalanced and they would have to send her away, to be cared for by experienced psychiatrists and doctors.

Later that night after Hugh had made some calls, Katherine was taken away. She had completely retreated into a world of silence and Jane couldn't help but feel sorry for her. Jane was there when Hugh dismissed Rhea, who quickly gathered her things and fled the house.

When they were alone in Brandon's room, Jane tucked the weary boy into his bed and Hugh leaned down and gently kissed his forehead. Tired as he was, Brandon managed to drape his arms across his father's neck and in that gesture was a forgiveness that touched Jane's heart.

Together, holding hands, Jane and Hugh stood there until Brandon had gone to sleep.

Then Hugh took Jane in his arms and his kiss was forceful and demanding. When they drew apart, Hugh said, "We have a lot of happy years ahead of us, my darling."

And Jane knew in her heart that she would look forward to them with Hugh at her side.